They
Too Know A
Thing Or
Two

Previous publications

Kaleidoscope of Living Thoughts

I'm Jane

Memory Rings The Bells

We two know a thing or two (Daisy and Poppette).

They Too Know
A Thing Or Two

Presented by
Betty and Ken Collins

Foreword by
Brian Davies I.F.A.W.

Regency Press (London & New York) Ltd.
125 High Holborn, London WC1V 6QA

ISBN 0 7212 0818 5

Printed and bound in Great Britain by
Buckland Press Ltd., Dover, Kent.

CONTENTS

FOREWORD

"They Too Know A Thing Or Two" will delight animal lovers everywhere. This compilation of poetry and prose, expresses such dedication and sympathy for our animal friends that I'm sure it will appeal to just about all who strive to protect animals world-wide.

Betty Collins speaks for our voiceless friends . . . not only to those of us who are already listening, but to those who have yet to hear.

For the animals,

BRIAN DAVIES,
Founder International Fund for Animal Welfare.

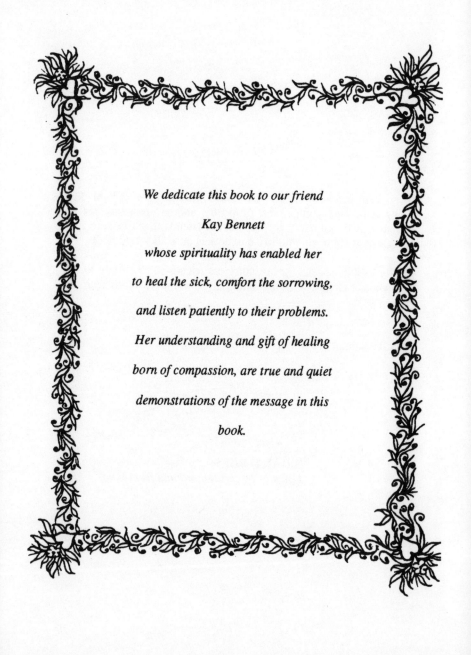

We dedicate this book to our friend

Kay Bennett

whose spirituality has enabled her

to heal the sick, comfort the sorrowing,

and listen patiently to their problems.

Her understanding and gift of healing

born of compassion, are true and quiet

demonstrations of the message in this

book.

MY INTRODUCTION AND EXPLANATION

This book is about people and animals – animals and people. It touches on many things and is yet about only one – an invitation to greater compassion. It presents some sad and painful facts and then turns the other cheek and offers humour in the belief that we cannot live a full life without seeing a funny side now and then. It asks questions and suggests some answers. It relates our own thinking to the thinking power of animals, and through those thoughts attempts to show a way of learning and teaching between the two. It is a glimpse of greater awareness and understanding towards progression for the human race and a kinder world for animals. It is a peep into greater happiness for all in the future – built on the backward glances of experience and a darker past, in order to learn a better way of life from those experiences – for what use is sorrow if we do not learn joy from the knowledge we have gained?

I cannot claim the inspiration for this book, it was more like an instruction to produce it. I can only explain that I received the material and wrote it down (in several different handwritings) often not knowing what I had written until I read it myself. Some aspects of the writing were outside my own knowledge as were some of the words used. These have all been checked and confirmed.

Obviously it has been necessary under such circumstances to tidy up the material received and amalgamate it into some sort of order. Other than that it is presented as it was received.

I am indebted to several kind friends for their help in this sorting and checking:- Richard and Jamie Middleton on bats and amphibians, Robert Lee B.Sc., M.R.C.V.S. on some veterinary items, Dorothy for her immaculate typing and correcting, Pearl for spotting my own many typing errors. My thanks are due also to my friends, Annabelle, Edna, Wendy, Ron, Pat and Alan for telling me about some of their own experiences, from which my spirit friends have been able to create some thoughtful lessons for our own use. Ken has given many hours of patient checking and tolerance, whilst I struggled with deciphering and anxious efforts to get it all right. My special thanks to Brian Davies for giving his valuable time and interest to write the Foreword.

In a book of this kind it is often difficult to find the dividing line between my own thoughts and spiritual guidance, but perhaps that is as it should be, for life on earth is in any case a mixture of both. Perhaps that in itself is an important message of this book, for universal acceptance of this fact would make a better, happier world for all life on it, people and animals alike. I hope you enjoy reading it, will find something helpful, something amusing within its pages and will be able to give some thought to any parts with which you may not at present agree. It is a wise soul that is willing to absorb knowledge, it is an even wiser soul that takes that knowledge from a wiser source than our own worldly thinking, for it lifts the mind to greater heights of appreciation, so that even our worst moments in life can be seen as opportunities for advancement. From this will be born a better, kinder world for both people and animals. For further information please read on, I wish you well and happiness in achievement, for your efforts could save much suffering – our purpose in presenting this book.

A KEY TO HEAVEN'S DOOR

If all the world would send a smile
    Instead of bombs and tears,
And everyone could laugh awhile
    Instead of hate and fears,
In place of horror, kindness given,
    The pain all eased away,
The angels then could smile in heaven,
    As we greet the joyful day
With happiness in every soul,
    Compassion in every heart,
A peaceful world our final goal,
    And now is the time to start.
For every thought of love we give,
    Is a gem that's heaven sent,
The shining moments we could live
    In this life that's only lent.
May every dark and cruel mind
    See compassion's guiding face,
And learn the joy of being kind –
    The entrance to heaven's grace.

A PLACE IN THE GARDEN

As the acreage of towns gradually increases, absorbing more and more of the countryside, we have to realise that the more we take for our own use, the less there is for the wildlife for whom the fields and hedgerows are home and source of food.

Even villages are spreading wider and wider as new houses, small estates and light industry claim their portion of the land. Mankind seems to be the only species of the world that does not suffer the threat of extinction through lack of numbers. While so many other inhabitants of the earth decline, homo sapiens increases at an extraordinary rate in spite of wars and diseases. History shows that these reductions in population are brought about by mankind itself, almost as if it is a subconscious effort to curb the problem of over population. If so, we do this just as badly and wastefully as we do a great many other things, for war and disease decimates the younger elements of mankind, and we have lost to a considerable extent the natural instincts that result in self-preservation of a species that occurs when nature's laws are obeyed.

Greed and materialistic thinking by too many people, set us on the wrong pathway so many years ago, that it has become increasingly difficult to rediscover and practise a more spiritual and humane way of life. Indeed the baser habits of mankind are often accepted now as the normal way of life, so that no effort is made to improve the general thinking of human beings that would lift humanity to a higher, kinder way of living.

It is an interesting reflection on our use of words, that our words human and humane, although derived from the same root, have very different meanings because of our own activities and thinking. Human we certainly are, humane we are not – as a species, in fact we are among the cruellest occupants of the planet earth.

Fortunately there are many kinder more unselfish minds amongst the sorrowing millions, who can and do hold high the torch of compassion, and however dark the outlook may be at times, these caring folk shine like a beacon from a hill top, and these are the souls that point the way that others may follow – these are the thinkers with the foresight and sensitivity that can actually rescue the world from its own self-destruction.

There is a bunch of keys that opens all doors towards this rescue. They are labelled compassion, kindness, love and spirituality. With these we can step from the darkness of despair, greed and selfishness into the light of true happiness around the world.

Is this task too large? Has the rot we have engendered gone too far? No, we are told it has not. Millions of kindly people everywhere put their compassionate thoughts into action, perhaps by their own individual efforts in daily life, maybe by supporting various charitable organisations or joining with others in actual physical efforts.

Many such kindly people channel those efforts into the use of their own gardens as miniature wildlife or bird sanctuaries, and this can be an important contribution for the protection of some species, especially as we have in fact helped ourselves to some of the terrain that was rightly theirs – it is the least we can do to compensate them to some degree.

It is important when undertaking this task, to create some kind of continuity. Animals, whether domestic or wild, are creatures of habit. If we create an artificial bird or animal housing estate or canteen, it must be done on a regular basis. Young birds learning to feed at our mini dining tables through the summer months, when we like to pop out into our gardens now and then, will die in the cold of winter if we do not stir ourselves to venture out in the frost or wet with our contributions of food at certain times of the day. Our own babies and young children learn survival by the pattern of the lives that we create, why should we expect the young of any other species to be different – especially as we do not credit them with our own powers of reasoning? Bird-tables, *not* within cat-jumping distance of a shed or fence, are ideal for many birds, but some, wagtails, wrens and blackbirds for instance prefer to find their food on the ground. Nestboxes strategically placed where predators cannot reach are another helpful way of compensating for loss of natural habitat, and the Royal Society for The Protection of Birds has helpful literature on all these points.

Butterflies are helped with many ordinary garden flowers and shrubs, such as buddleia, broom, heaths and heathers, lavender, primroses, pink ice plants and single Michaelmas daisies, whilst many wild flowers also attract them. Eggs may not be laid on the same plants that provide food for the butterflies, and it is worth the effort to find out the ones that are native to your own area and their preferences for food and breeding sites.

Hedgehogs like warm boxes under compost heaps during the winter, or will tuck under garden sheds with suitable bedding. They can be fed tinned dog or cat food through spring and summer – *not* as so many people believe with bread and milk. If you collect heaps of rubbish to burn in your garden, always make sure your prickly friend is not hiding inside before you set fire to it, and if you use a garden fork or spade on your heap, remember the possible lodger underneath it, it is a valuable pest controller – it can also feel pain.

There is no place in a garden sanctuary for chemical pest control. If you manage your garden without these things, bees will reward your efforts with their pollination activities, especially amongst your peas, beans and tomatoes. You can all too easily cause their deaths with the wrong sprays. Slug pellets can take their toll of bird life, and your garden sanctuary becomes a death trap instead, to say nothing of possible disasters with pets – just ask any vet!

The birds and animals of our gardens need soil and grass, rocks that accommodate the insects, shrubs in which to hide, berries on which to feed, so let us not smother the ground with concrete, or prune away the berries and seeds. Let us find an odd corner for the wild flowers, a few nettles, thistles or thrift plants for instance that are so valuable to our wildlife, remember they are not weeds to a butterfly. Then we can truly provide a place in the garden for some of those friends that share this world with us.

TWO LITTLE LADYBIRDS

Two little ladybirds were sitting on a rose,
What they were doing there, goodness only knows,
But when they had finished it, their spots were all aglow
And a thousand baby ladybirds were on their way to show –
Why two little ladybirds never can say "No"!

So when the ladybirds have lived their little lives right through,
They'll carry on, their service give, just like me and you.
They'll fly away to heaven of course, and join the other few
Who left a legacy of spots to find a rose or two,
For without these happy ladybirds, what would our roses do?

A MORNING PRAYER

Please protect us through this day,
That we may walk the Spirit way,
To help all animals to share
The love we have, that we may care
For all the creatures of the world,
Compassion's flag to be unfurled.

Please grant the wisdom of your love,
The sickness of our world to solve,
Compassion guide our erring minds,
Creating hope that never ends,
That all the peoples of the earth
Will understand compassion's worth.

May all our planet's wondrous life
Be free of pain and earthly strife,
Please help us move this earthly dream
To the glory of a sunrise gleam,
To make this world a kinder place,
Through the loving call of the human race.

Help us know the power of prayer,
For all God's creatures everywhere.
Please help us make all turmoil cease,
That all the world may live in peace,
In gratitude for life on earth,
Progressing to our heavenly birth.

A TALE OF THREE TAILS

The largest of these three tails is long, strong and golden. It can sway gently from side to side in a dignified fashion or swing wildly round and round. It can also beat a rhythm on the floor or whip enthusiastically from left to right and right to left and hit any handy human behind the knees, causing their collapse if they were not ready for it. This same tail can sweep almost anything from a coffee table with one swipe, or waggle gently at the tip when its owner is feeling coy. It belongs to an outsize Golden Labrador called Barney, whose best friends own the other two tails.

These are very short indeed with untidy little tassels on the ends. They are nowhere near as versatile as Barney's tail, and have only two speeds and directions – very slow and very fast, and up and down or sideways. If the sideways movement combines with very fast the whole rear end will wag with it, giving an impression of dogs with a head and tail at each end. This can be confusing if you are trying to pick them up, which will be quite often as the owners of these two tails are tiny Yorkshire Terriers – roughly about the side of Barney's head, though Poppette is only about half the weight of her companion Daisy.

They delight in walking about underneath their Labrador friend, confusing him as to which foot they are running round, and standing on their hind feet to touch noses with him – perhaps they come from Eskimo stock, where I believe it is traditional to greet in this way. Barney for his part has always been careful not to tread on Poppette and Daisy, and has always put up with their puppy antics with good grace and dignity. Now that they are in the prime of life and Barney is reaching more mature years, the girls are a little more respectful some of the time, whilst he is as tolerant and eager to greet them as ever he was.

It gives us food for thought, that here is a dog of great power dealing with such tiny companions in such a gentle, tolerant way, when he could in fact crush them with one snap of powerful jaws or one blow of a mighty paw. Instead he rises above the situation and welcomes them as friends. They in their turn, welcome him and are unafraid – they know they can trust their massive friend, so peace prevails. If only members of the human race could follow suit – trust and be trusted, no matter where the strength and power lies – what a happy world it would be, a sobering thought prompted by one labrador dog and two Yorkshire Terriers – three tails all wagging with the joy of meeting, with three different tales to tell.

These three bring another thought for consideration, to challenge our knowledge and open our minds to greater possibilities. When Poppette and Daisy are being taken by car to visit Barney and our friends – his owners, Poppette in particular knows where she is going before we tell her or mention Barney's name – we dare not if we are to keep the journey peaceful. She may have been asleep for an hour, but wakens and shows her enthusiasm as we near our friends' home. He on the other hand has been told of our visit, and occupies his time looking expectantly out of the window, or laying down with ears alert for the sound of the car that will bring his mischievous friends. Some kind of telepathy would appear to be the answer, but does Poppette collect the thought from us as we drive along, or from Barney at his window, watching with patient anticipation? He has been known to do this even when his owners did not know we were on the way to visit them, could he have been picking up the thought from Poppette whom we would have told in this instance? It would seem impossible to prove any of these theories, but there has to be some explanation, and we who think we know so much, can find we know so little, because of three happy dogs with three such different tails.

THERE'S NO STING IN THIS TALE

It had been a hot dry summer and our plants and shrubs were surviving only because of our efforts with the water waste from household chores.

Our short row of runner beans seemed particularly appreciative, and our careful attention, together with that of a sundry collection of flying insects, honey and bumble bees, produced a welcome crop of runner beans – until the weather began to change. A few showers, some high winds, and the bees virtually disappeared. For two whole days I didn't see a single bee and bean flowers lay scattered on the ground like red confetti.

On the third day, as I half-heartedly worked my way around the bean flowers with my tickling stick (a blackbird feather) in an attempt to rectify the inattention of the insects, I spied just one lonely bumble bee who seemed to find the magnitude of the task all too much for her. I remarked upon the situation to her in fact, because it was all too obvious that the response to her efforts would be very limited indeed. So I suggested that she ask her friends and relations to come along and help, as we sorely needed their attentions to our beans. I don't mind admitting now that I more or less pleaded with her to bring further bee company.

She flew away as I fetched more water to the cause, and I thought no more about it for the rest of the day, except that in passing en route to the compost bin on several occasions, I still noted that no bees were present.

The next day however, it was a very different story as dozens of bumble bees busied themselves amongst the flowers. I can never remember seeing so many or so much industry on one short row of anything as I did that day. The results were spectacular!

Clusters of runner beans began to hang once more amongst the green leaves of summer. They grew long and succulent, supplying all our needs and more in no time at all. The mad rush of bees of that one day didn't continue, it settled down to a nice steady, normal visitation, which kept our supply at an easy, manageable pace.

You can make of this little tale what you will, and find any interpretation that you wish for the rescue of our runner bean crop. For my part, I thanked the bumble bees for coming, because I noticed no honey bees amongst them, and it is a fact that country folk, who are noted for their gardening expertise, have talked to the bees since time immemorial, it is one of the basics of folklore gardening. Anyway – I personally think it best to be on the safe side, for it can do no harm, so long as you are careful who you tell about the birds and bees, for some human companions would never understand and might even scorn your experience. On the other hand, maybe they either don't like runner beans, or perhaps like them and envy your success. You must make up your own mind about this little tale, but I know who I'll be chatting up when I next find red confetti on the ground, and who knows what unseen and unknown power may be at work along with the busy bees.

THE ROAD OF COMPASSION

Some of us mere human beings know about the pain and frustrations of trying to help animals, our so-called lesser brethren. Those who have the spirituality and inclination to tackle the problems of cruelty, hopelessness and neglect, often find themselves in heartbreaking situations. They steel themselves to cope with situations they would rather avoid and sometimes actions they would never contemplate in the ordinary way, perhaps by ending an animal's earthly life because that drastic solution is the kindest in the end. Sometimes there are no options, or all are undesirable, and someone has to make a decision.

Heartbreak circumstances are liable to arise for anyone trying to express their spirituality through animals, and anyone who cannot either physically or emotionally deal with it, should perhaps be confining the activity to a supporting role (and this too is much needed), or even trying a different pathway of life. In one way or another it may not be the right time for such testing and challenge. The rocky road of helping and rescuing animals from the cruel and unthinking acts of mankind, is for the strong in body, mind and spirit. Only those with such strength can ever succeed, and failure can cause further suffering to both animal and would-be rescuer.

This pattern can be observed from the comparatively simple act of offering a good home to an unwanted animal, to vast rescue operations on an international scale. Yet these are ways in which many people develop their own spirituality in a very positive way. Warnings of possible difficulties do not deter, fear of the trials ahead are laid aside in grim determination to play a part in reducing suffering in the animal world. Those who choose this route to God are often unsung heroes of our world. Other acts of mercy are frequently recognised, acclaimed and even rewarded, whilst those who tread the path of animal rescue are often overlooked, unrewarded and sometimes regarded as cranky or a nuisance by those whose own spiritual achievements are so unhappily low that they do not even have the eyes to recognise the work of God when they see it through service to animals.

During my own sojourn on earth, I have adopted three adult animals. The first of these was a beautiful blue/grey and white cat. She came to me because we had inherited mice in our new home, and the smallholding that had been her own previous home in wild moorland was having to be abandoned. My own less isolated smallholding at least provided some of the conditions to which she was accustomed, but she always retained a wild streak whilst availing herself of our hospitality. Her short thick velvety fur made me think that a Russian Blue was somewhere in her distant parentage, and it was a great temptation to stroke that soft inviting coat, but although she was happy to curl up on any handy lap in front of a blazing log fire, and would purr loudly, she strongly objected to the intimacy of stroking and would whip round to grab the offending hand in both front paws, with claws extended just enough to get the message across without any actual harm. This cat certainly *did* know a thing or two! She daily delivered a present of a dead mouse or rat, depositing it on the back doorstep, and creating a noise that was a cross between a meow and a yell until I went to inspect the offering, only then would she take it away. She never to my knowledge caught a bird, and I suspect she was clever enough to bring her catches for me to see in order to justify her existence with us and the comfortable home we gave her. On the other hand perhaps I do her an injustice, maybe it was a sort of feline 'thank you'. It was a satisfactory arrangement for all concerned.

One problem with adopting an adult cat, can be its tendency to associate itself with a particular territory rather than people. This can mean their refusal to settle in a new home, and they have been known to travel many miles back to their old haunts. I feared that Muffy might do just that because her old home was only a few miles away and finding it would have been quite easy for a cat of this character. A wise elderly lady of the village advised me to smear a little butter on her paws as this would prevent her roaming. I wonder if this is the origin of the colloquial phrase to 'butter someone up'? I did as advised, and can only report without theorising, that she never went away. Ask about this of a veterinary surgeon if you are adopting an adult cat! There is no scientific evidence for this traditional country trick, but most country folk know it can work, and if the vet knows enough about people as well as animals, he will smile and say "Well it won't harm the cat, so if you want to try it, by all means have a go, but watch your carpet!" Maybe there *is* a cat somewhere who doesn't respond to the butter treatment, but I have never personally heard of one that didn't happily sit and lick the unexpected treat from its paws, and then stay firmly put!

My second adoption was Penny, a Yorkshire Terrier of about three years. She came from a nice family of Mum, Dad, two little girls and a baby boy of crawling age. It seemed that the daughters were quite acceptable to Penny, for most little girls harbour enough early mothering instinct to want to cuddle and be kind to their pets. Little boys alas are often more aggressive, and this little one saw Penny as a handy target. Being smaller, Penny's only defences were either flight or fight. Flight being difficult within the confines of a home, fight was the only option left. If I felt that a bit of basic early training was called for towards this baby bulldozer with fur pulling tendencies, it was not for me to say, it was merely part of my job to find new homes for animals in need of them, and this one came to mine.

Penny settled quite well with us, although it was all of six months before we'd sorted out all her little whims and fancies. She would prick up her ears and stare hard and wide-eyed at any passing man of the six foot plus of her previous master. I often wondered what she was thinking – did she feel abandoned by him? I'll never ever know how she felt.

Penny was eleven years old before we had to save her the trauma and pain of incurable illness. We loved her from the start and she soon learned to return the compliment with all the winning ways of her breed and become a close companion of my mother. That family will never know what they missed, but their loss was our gain, and I think Penny's too.

My third attempt to adopt was an unwanted dog, and I have to admit to total failure, a fact that I shall always regret. The only plus to this one is that the last ten days of its life were happy ones for him, perhaps the only happy days of his whole eighteen months of life. Fred was a beautiful but skinny Alsatian, with light golden head and legs, with the usual black and grey on his back. I remember thinking that his name didn't suit him at all, and over the ten days he was with us, I gradually changed his name to Sherry because of his colour. He didn't seem to mind, I suspect he would have answered to anyone who was kind to him no matter what they called him.

Unfortunately, after he had been with us a week, he began to show aggressive tendencies towards my parents and visitors to our home, but complete and utter devotion to me who had rescued him. He was afraid of a number of things, especially walking sticks and newspapers, obviously having been on the wrong end of these sometime during his short life. But my father had to use a walking stick to get about and was in the habit of tucking his newspaper under his arm as he moved about the bungalow. Seeing and knowing the danger signs, I began to fear for his future with us. We discovered that ours was his fourth home so here was a dog that had not had the advantage of any stability in life, must often have been hungry, judging by the condition of his coat and body, and had never had any real affection shown to him nor accepted from him.

At the end of ten days his ribs were no longer showing, his coat was groomed and sleek and he virtually worshipped the ground I walked on, waiting in the window for my return from work each day, refusing – my mother said – to even go out into the garden for natural purposes. The crisis came when a friend who was visiting us tried to protect him from a bumble bee, using her magazine. Sherry, mistaking her intention for an attack on him, went for her, and only my anticipation and quick intervention prevented a nasty situation. It was clearly not safe to leave Sherry with my elderly parents, and after consultation with several vets, it became obvious that so much expert training would be required to get him over these fears, that it was not possible for me to do it myself, and in any case I did not have the necessary experience or knowledge. It would have been unkindness in the extreme to pass him on to yet another home while he was being trained, with no guarantee that the training would make him any happier even if it did make him more manageable. Sherry had learnt to love and trust me during our short friendship, and it was I who had to spare him any further distress. I had to love him enough to end his earthly life while he was experiencing the only happiness he had ever known. It was the hardest decision I have ever had to make. I have never regretted that decision but have always regretted that I could not give him the long joyful life that he deserved. One of my life's failures, with only his last ten days of contentment and the devotion he was so pleased to give as compensation.

The problems that animals have are nearly always the result of the activities of the human race in some way or other. Sometimes he breeds weaknesses into a strain, purely to get some advantage for himself, or maybe just to conform to a fashion. It is often seen in pedigree dogs and horses. Other animals suffer from either cruelty or ignorance at the hands of mankind and each animal will respond to that treatment in its own individual way. Some will be cowed, some will become angry in self defence, the same sort of responses in fact that would be expected from the human species in similar circumstances, but *they* are not so much at the mercy of their fellow human beings as their animal counterparts.

However, there are many success stories for those who try to help the animal kingdom. Two good friends of mine adopted a poodle, one of several dogs they helped through the years. The owner of this one had gone into hospital and was not expected to be able to look after it. In spite of all their efforts, the dog would not settle, but they had the bright idea of trying to trace the previous owner to see if there was any hope of the dog returning to its original home. Their efforts succeeded. Not only was the lady at home again, but well enough to look after a dog, and because she missed her pet so much was about to get another one! Instead, poodle and owner were touchingly reunited, my friends left the dog's new basket and other paraphernalia with which they had tried to comfort the dog whilst in their care, with the owner. All the problems, expense and distress that my friends had experienced, had led to a happy reunion that made all their efforts worth while, as foster owners for a little time in the life of that dog.

This sort of situation always suggests some other unseen guiding hand – a hand attached to knowledge that we mortals do not have, or did the dog in its own psychic way know it could return and that the separation was only temporary? I believe that both explanations may have some truth in them. I think the dog could have known with that sixth sense that is a gift to many animals and human beings alike, but that the guiding hand of spirit friends brought about the circumstances that led to the dog's return. My friends had to have the inspirational thought to find the owner and the tenacity to follow it through. Maybe their own psychic sixth sense was also working overtime towards this grand reunion. However you look at it, the result was a happy ending to a sad little situation, a service given freely, a working arm for Spirit.

Such acts of compassion are carried out in their millions throughout the world, by individual people who choose to tread the spiritual path in this particular way, although in most cases they may not think of the service as part of spirituality, but that does not matter, labels often don't. The two main points are, that all these people are quietly furthering their own spiritual progression with completely unselfish motives and in the process are reducing the sum total of animal suffering.

. On a national and international level, organisations both large and small, are tackling the problems on an enormous scale. The International Fund for Animal Welfare, The Royal Society for the Prevention of Cruelty to Animals, The Canine Defence League and The Cats Protection League, plus many others, are all committed to reducing animal suffering on a huge scale. There are in fact hundreds of them struggling against apathy, lack of sufficient funds and simple straightforward ignorance of the subject.

There are organisations to protect almost every form of animal life from elephants to butterflies, and a veritable army of caring people willing to devote their lives towards this end.

The people who choose to be involved with the working end of this enormous task, are special people. Their compassion knows no bounds, but it has to be a love through strength of mind and courage. It is not enough for them to cuddle a fluffy puppy or kitten. If it needs help they have to give it, if their dedication means seeing flowing blood and mutilation, they see it and act, even if at first they are physically sickened by the sight, even if they often despair. Sometimes it means taking criticism or ridicule from other people, for there are many people who quite sincerely feel that money, time and effort should not be expended on animals while so many people, especially children are suffering so much throughout the world. Mrs. Maria Dicken, founder of the People's Dispensary for Sick Animals, probably got it right when she insisted that she was not asking people to help animals *instead* of people, she was asking that animals be helped *as well* rather than not at all.

We have come a long way since 1917 when Mrs Dicken had such foresight and made her forthright statement, and thanks to the hard work and dedication of people in the front line of animal welfare, enlightenment has dawned and becomes ever brighter with their efforts and of those who support them with words, deeds and cash. As more and more people become aware of beauty in nature – conscious of their natural environment and the need to protect it, then compassion for the plight of animals will gradually increase, and every individual who adds their own contribution plays an important part.

That compassion will increase by leaps and bounds as more people realize the spiritual significance of that caring, not only towards the human race, but also the animals who are also a part of Spirit. They also know pain, love and rejection, happiness and despair. Compassion isn't an easy road, but the best things in life are those that are earned. Sometimes, just giving an ill-treated dog or cat a happy home can *be* that hard earned reward. But the real compensations are the spiritual experience gained and the gratitude in the eyes of a rescued animal, for they know compassion when they see it.

FIRES OF COMPASSION

Do not despair for the sadness that you hear and see,
For other sights and sounds spell out tranquillity.
Do not weep for pain that others know,
But gird your mind and heart to the ebb and flow
Of passion's help and rescue, reaching out
Towards the blending of pure love and thought.
The burning fears that lay all creatures low
From cruel unthinking act or mortal blow
Can purify another heart and gentler mind,
That searching souls may ever seek and find
The fires that light the way for kindly action,
And from the smouldering ashes, rise compassion
Towards a kinder better world of loving peace,
That cruelty and pain may one day cease.
Without the pain, compassion is not born,
And kindness never sees the Light of dawn,
But when the fire of true compassion lights the world,
The truth of God's own love will be unfurled
To shine beyond our poor imagination,
And grant to us His perfect inspiration,
That life be free of cruel pain and sorrow,
Compassion lead the way to heaven's bright tomorrow.

HELP!

Whilst it is always sensible to be cautious of an animal that you don't know – one which of course would not know you either – some people are unnecessarily afraid of animals that could not harm them anyway. They completely overlook the fact that the animal may be afraid of the human being, especially as people often express their fears in strange ways that must be quite incomprehensible to an animal. The only advantage to be found in this situation, is that it can often be the source of a smile or two:–

What's that lady doing
    Standing on a chair?
There must be something brewing,
    'Cos she's tearing at her hair,
I wish she'd stop that screaming,
    I must cover up my ears,
I hope she isn't dreaming
    Of nasty creepy fears.

She's looking up to heaven,
    Then looking down at me,
That's another yell she's given,
    Whatever can she see?
People are such funny things
    To have around the house,
I s'pose its 'cos the're human beings,
    That they fright' a poor wee mouse!

PRIDE ON FOUR LEGS

False pride in members of the human race is considered something to be avoided – a sin of the soul to be avoided at all costs, for when pride goes over the top or appears for the wrong reasons it becomes vanity.

Vanity and false pride seem to be unknown to the animal kingdom, demonstrating that there is a state of life where they have the edge over us. It is surprising how much we can learn from animals when we begin to dig deeply into their natures – the real animal behind the furry face and outstretched paw. It is then, if we are truthful with ourselves, that we have to humbly admit that we still have much to learn or perhaps regain, and animals can be a source of inspiration towards more spiritual thinking.

Domesticated animals often exhibit a proper pride that is quite uncontaminated with false concepts, and has nothing in common with the kind of vanity which seems to be confined to the human race.

This situation suggests that false pride is not something we are born with, but a fault we have acquired through the years. Some might feel they can blame the environment of their own upbringing for this rather silly streak in their natures. But then one is bound to observe that not all people brought up in an atmosphere of false pride acquire this way of looking at life, and of course, a pet animal living in the same atmosphere from an early age will not develop the trait either. We are then forced to the conclusion that this fault in human nature, along with all the others, is a weakness of each individual that exhibits it – a lesson of life to be learnt, a character to be strengthened and developed through its present earthly life.

The earthly conditions in which such a person finds himself, that seemed to encourage false pride, may well be a testing for that soul, a challenge to overcome the difficulty. Those who fail now will have another opportunity, those who succeed will be well equipped to face the next. Domestic animals appear to have the knowledge already, it does not seem to be a lesson they have to learn, which does suggest that in this respect those animals demonstrate a superiority.

Most animals do, however, possess a true pride of their own, which is demonstrated in many different ways according to species, and quite clearly has nothing to do with its upbringing. See the magnificent pride of a wild stallion as he stands supreme in his native wildness. Observe the same proud supremacy of a trained shire horse as he too stands with quiet dignity, master of all he surveys, knowing his own great strength and rightly proud of it, only using it for the controlled demands of a human master. These two very different kinds of horse demonstrate their own special kinds of pride. From basically similar backgrounds but with the added consideration that one is completely wild, the other domesticated and trained by man, they have different experiences of life. No matter what you do to these animals they retain that special mark of true pride. Would that we humans could retain our own pride under adverse conditions. A few can, most cannot.

Cats are well known for their pride in cleanliness and appearance. They will wash and clean themselves to an extreme. Try stroking a cat whilst it is grooming itself and it will usually start cleaning enthusiastically where you have touched it, obviously feeling that you have soiled that particular spot with your hand. You meant well of course, but you have momentarily soiled your cat and upset its pride and the cleaning and smoothing of its coat must be done again. When a cat fails to exhibit pride in its appearance, there is either something wrong with it or it is getting too old to care. Some people are like that too!

Most females with young exhibit pride in their offspring, and this applies to people, and animals in the wild as well as our domestic pets. We have the opportunity to see these things on our television screens, even though we may not be safari types who delight in wending our way through jungle conditions ourselves. To see Mum Lioness emerge with her cubs for the first time is something special, her protection and pride are obvious. To watch our own dog or cat doing the same thing leaves no doubt about their pride in their offspring. Our pets will make quite sure we witness and approve the new family.

All this is a natural pride in achievement to all life of more evolved thinking, including the human race. But sometimes domesticated animals will take their pride a step further and show pride and express pleasure at a more artificial achievement.

I once borrowed two beautiful Afghan Hounds to use on the stage. It was a music hall kind of production, called Gaslight Gaieties. A bunch of St. Trinian type schoolgirls with wrinkled stockings, tatty panama hats and bloomers at half mast had been singing "Daddy Wouldn't Buy Me a Bow-wow", but an effective exit for the girls was proving difficult. They were so good in their cheeky representation of the little horrors, that to merely walk off the stage would have been an anti-climax indeed. It was decided that I should walk on with these two aristocrats of the dog world, myself dressed in an elegant Edwardian gown complete with cart-wheel hat. I merely had to pause long enough to metaphorically turn up my nose at the scruffy schoolgirls, walk past them and exit upstage, the girls following me, aping the hobble skirt walk and my disdainful attitude. The owner warned me to keep moving if by chance the audience should applaud our entrance, for these were champion dogs, used to winning, and receiving a clapping reception at dog shows. Their owner felt sure that such a reception would prompt the dogs to stop and enjoy the acclaim on our stage, in which case I might have difficulty in moving them on in keeping with my stage attire and Edwardian demeanour!

The audience loved the scruffy girls and also the spectacular appearance of these two prima donnas on four feet. They brought the house down, stopped and wouldn't move until the clapping began to die down. I was forced to bow to the wills of these lovely animals until, pride satisfied, we were able to make our dignified exit as planned. The girls enlarged their act with their own genuine laughter. It was quite clear that the dogs enjoyed every minute of their glory, and they did it at every performance!

When animals actually act on a stage and enjoy their performance without human bribery or force, we have to accept that they can experience pride in achievement, which has nothing in common with the vanity we can feel as pride in possessions or feelings of superiority.

Genuine, simple pride in achievement for either ourselves or others for the right reasons promotes endeavour, and endeavour promotes achievement – a circle of qualities that can spiral us to ever greater heights of understanding of life, both this one and the next. The key is the humbleness of pride in achievement, the pride without vanity that is part of the knowledge of animals. Pride on four legs could teach much to those of us with only two.

A CURRICULUM OF ANIMALS

It is a curious fact of life, that amongst the animal lovers of the world there are three distinct types that stand out for all to see and recognise:- Cat lovers, dog lovers and the horsey ones.

The first two are quite specific and rarely wander over to the other species. Although they may have pets of both kinds, preference for one will predominate.

Horse lovers on the other hand will frequently share their affections with a dog, although here again, if forced to make a choice, their first love will probably remain with the horse. It is a more shadowy area of mankind's relationship with domestic animals, for in this case the horse is likely to be giving a service as well as affection and loyalty. To a lesser degree the dog that is owned by such a person will also be displaying the attribute of service, all of which helps to prove the point that these sections of animal owners are all very different kinds of people.

As a matter of fact the animals themselves give the indication of the differences. People own horses, dogs own people and cats condescend to accept people, and quite easily go and live elsewhere if they feel so inclined.

The home they leave behind may have nothing wrong as a home – indeed it could be a very good home, but cats prefer to retain their freedom to choose, whilst dogs will do the best they can with what they've got and give their loyalty even in adverse conditions. Their affection may have to be earned and returned, but their loyalty is given freely. Most dog owners who truly love their pets will agree that much of their own activity revolves around what they can or cannot do because of their dog.

A dog will rarely abandon its home, whilst cats can do so quite easily. I once had a lovely cat myself that suddenly went to live next door for no apparent reason, except perhaps that I had two other cats and my neighbour had none. Perhaps he felt he was filling a gap in their lives, and for all I know he was, because they did seem to enjoy his company. Some cats will trick two different people or families into thinking they own them, sharing their lives between people living a short distance from each other, benefiting from the food and comforts provided by both households, a sort of feline insurance policy. Cats certainly know a thing or two, preserving an independence that helps them survive all kinds of adverse conditions. The dog's loyalty to its master can be its undoing if that master or mistress does not have the same loyalty towards the dog.

The horse on the other hand, does not seem to have the same *instinctive* loyalty of the dog, nor the same independence of the cat. It has to be trained if it is to be of use to mankind either in service or in the capacity of a pet. Its sheer size and strength demands discipline, otherwise it might as well be on the plains of wild horse country. But once it has been moulded into the ways of mankind, it can be a most rewarding animal to have around. Many have learnt loyalty and affection on the way, and its strength and power has proved its worth over aeons of time. But through all those years of manipulation, the horse has somehow managed to retain many qualities that are instinctive to it. Its love of freedom remains, compared to the dog's ability to give it up for its owner. The ability of the horse to learn, compares favourably with the dog but has nothing in common with the cat that normally refuses to learn anything it doesn't want to.

Whilst we ponder on the facts of ownership and learning between man and animals, perhaps we should come to the conclusion that we learn more from them than we could ever teach them. We may consider ourselves superior, but it is a sobering thought that in addition to satisfying some of our practical needs, we need the teaching the animals can give us. Their only need of *our* teaching to *them* is that they can be of service to us and fit into our human way of life.

When we do this kindly and with understanding, it can be of benefit to all. When we lose compassion as our motivation, we are taking retrograde steps that bring disaster to our own spiritual progress, with pain and misery to the animals. It is all too easy to consider ourselves so superior to the animal kingdom, better that knowledge, space and loyalty be shared, so that we may all play a worthy part in life on the earth, for 'someone up there' knows just what we do and think and what our motives are. Let these things be worthy of the animals in our care. Let not their trust be betrayed by egoistical mankind, nor trust in our own consciences be betrayed by that ego.

THE GIFT OF TIME

How many people, when faced with a task they don't really want to do, say to themselves (and often other people) "I haven't got time"? It would be easier to count the ones that never make this time-honoured excuse. It is rarely true, and in our heart of hearts we know it is not so. It is our own selection of priorities.

The truth of the matter is that in this modern world, we have become obsessed with speed, that will-o-the-wisp that certainly has its uses, many drawbacks, and which mankind has elevated into an almost god-like status. Nearly everything and anything has to be done at the double, except the things we don't really want to do anyway. This thief of time robs us of many opportunities to do worthwhile things – perhaps giving a helping hand wherever it may be needed, a neighbour or elderly person struggling with some problem that is beyond their capabilities. Maybe we fail to write a cheque to help some worthy cause, or write an anxiously awaited letter. Perhaps we procrastinate to the point of no return at times, fail to mend the garden shed or allow the weeds to turn our garden into a mini jungle – nice for the wildlife but not for the neighbours. Our excuses are endless and by that procrastination we make life so complicated for ourselves that in the end we really do not have sufficient time for all the tasks we either meant, need or should do. We are in a time trap of our own making, one trap into which animals do not fall – they are too wise!

As a result of this mismanagement of our time, we become overstressed, short tempered, and above all we rob ourselves of the time to 'stand and stare'. This is something that should be part of everyone's daily curriculum, for a pause in the rush of our daily activities to simply stare and inwardly digest the right kind of view, is a healing and uplifting habit, to put it at its most modest level. At a higher level it can teach and lift the mind beyond our wildest dreams, develop progression for the soul and give us a peep into the world of spirit that gives us strength, hope and peace of mind – a mild meditation.

Ideally this view should be something that appeals to us personally and artistically, perhaps green fields, woodlands, gardens or the sea. For others the ideal restful scene may be mist on the river or reflections on a still lake – whatever touches that inner appreciation that we all have tucked away somewhere. All have their own particular idea of beauty that appeals to different people with different ideas. But these things are not always possible, and it is fortunate for us that we can find upliftment in many other aspects of nature, so that we can study and appreciate one single flower that can stir the sleeping mind and feed a tired soul. One single tree can have the same effect. The world of animals too can provide that link with nature and the unseen healing power. To watch in wonder a butterfly or bird, and truly see its mystery and link with God, can sometimes do more good to us than all the pills and potions, and infinitely less harm than many of them. It is an instinctive knowledge in the animal kingdom that we would do well to recapture, for mankind once knew about these things and used them, before he allowed his brain to override that inbuilt knowledge, instead of working with both – side by side.

Even pictures of flowers, trees and animals can be a help to relieve the stresses of daily living, but to actually watch a bird in flight or an animal in graceful movement can do much more. To touch and stroke an animal gently is known to have therapeutic value, just sharing briefly the wonder of time with an animal at peace with itself, can heal and uplift wilting or overstrung hearts and minds and nervous systems.

The animal kingdom knows very well about its own rhythms of life, each one conforming to the pattern of living that was given to it in the first place. It is we with our superior knowledge and advanced discoveries, who have in the process lost the true value of time and rhythm, manipulated it for our own use and fancy.

We upset the growth rate of crops and vegetation and interfere with the growth rate of farm animals and their breeding cycles, all in order to increase our own profits. Carelessly we alter nature's perfect timing without thought of the eventual consequences. The more we invent equipment to save ourselves time and effort, the less we seem to know about the best way to use the time and effort we have saved. Consequently we grossly misuse them in order to pander to our foolish ways.

Greed is often a driving force as we gather around us more and more of the things we think we want, rather than the things we know we need. In the end these accumulated possessions become a burden. In order to protect and look after them we have to use our precious time, thought and often money as well. All three could be put to better purpose if we really thought about it. An old 'Gentleman of the Road' once said to me many years ago – "I never worry about thieves and robbers, I have nothing for them to steal" – and I can still remember his quiet contented smile as he said it. He had however paused in his wanderings to share his few words of wisdom with me, perhaps his only possession – time well spent.

This man's way of life obviously gave him plenty of opportunities to stand and stare, and of course it would not be practical for most of us, nevertheless he well demonstrated the principle.

Most of us subconsciously feel that we each have our allotted span, and so we try to cram as much into it as possible, as if we were going on holiday and feel we must squash as many items into our suitcase as we possibly can, even though we won't need them all. This can crush and spoil the contents, make the case unnecessarily heavy to carry and runs the risk of bursting the locks of the case. Aren't we metaphorically doing these things with our lives? – packing too much into them, more in fact than we need, perhaps spoiling some aspects of our gift of life and burdening ourselves with too heavy a load.

Perhaps it is time to slow our daily lives a little, just enough to give us time to stand and stare with a few moments of our precious time. Then perhaps we would have the time to learn something worthwhile from nature – of which we are an integral part. Perhaps we would have time to share a little more of our thoughts and actions with others who may be in desperate need of those gifts, for the gift of time to us, is the gift that God meant us to use wisely, well and unselfishly. *Our* gift of time to *others* is the greatest gift that we can offer to people and animals in need. It embraces all other gifts, and is an expression of love that all can recognise, it can heal, uplift or even save a life, that precious gift of time.

THE GIFT OF SEASONS

When nature stirs the buds of spring
To bring new life to everything,
She clothes the trees with leafy green,
The finest gown you've ever seen
Sprinkled with flowers of gold and blue,
Mixed with every magic hue –
God's gift of springtime hope.

When nature spreads her summer glory,
To tell the world her splendid story
Of life in bloom to pure perfection,
Riots of colour for our selection,
From flame that's borrowed from the sun
To purest white the flowers come,
God's gift of summer splendour.

When nature drops her autumn leaves,
To toss them lightly on a breeze,
Drifting into hidden places,
With golden carpeting it graces
Every path in forest glade,
Dappled by the sun and shade,
God's gift of autumn glory.

When nature sleeps her winter days,
And jangling winds are songs of praise
Driving the snow in drifts of white,
To gleam and shine with the moon at night,
Peeping towards the spring ahead,
Reviving all that seemed so dead,
God's gift of winter rest.

And so the seasons wend their way,
Through every year and every day,
Teaching people of the earth
The lessons of all life's rebirth,
Changing with the march of time
According to His laws sublime,
God's gift of endless life.

Springtime pussy,
Summer beech,
In this world
To give and teach.

Autumn Acorns,
Winter holly,
Help us smile
And keep us jolly!

ANECDOTES ON A FELINE THEME

Cats have been feared or revered since time immemorial. They have been harbingers of good and bad luck according to colour or behaviour, and credited with psychic power to a very considerable degree. There are tales about cats that live within every strata of human company, from Queens to witches. They have been killed, cuddled and castrated, to meet the needs of the human race.

We cannot say these people owned cats, or that the cats owned people – as in the case of dogs – for cats are independent creatures who condescend to live with people and graciously accept their hospitality. In return they will catch a mouse or two, even rats where these are available – I had one once that tackled a stoat. They will decorate the hearthrug, add an air of mystery to the home and create a quietly interesting atmosphere of peaceful relaxation. All these things are helpful to people, and cats consider we should be grateful for these services.

There is of course another side to cats, they can be aggravating and try our patience. Cats, being rather fastidious in their habits, dig little holes in the garden for toilet purposes, carefully covering the spot they have used. But for some reason they do not seem to understand about seeds or gardeners' pride, and will choose the fine tilth the gardener has carefully prepared for a seed bed, usually with the seeds already in it. This to any true gardener is tantamount to a naughty child poking its tongue out.

After some cheeky indulgence in an activity that it knows displeases, a cat will often seek out its human companion, and offer a silent meow or rub around their legs whilst purring loudly. This can only be interpreted as a kind of challenge, defying you to be cross. Cats will take this attitude much further and reveal a superior sense of humour by offering to guide you to their scene of action. Their powers of telepathy are quite sufficient to get the message to us. Most people with cats will have been persuaded by puss to go out into the garden or maybe kitchen to view the dead mouse or bird that has been brought especially for your inspection. But most cats do not understand why we praise them for the mouse or rat and scold them for the bird. This seems to be about the only area where *we* could teach *them* a thing or two. For the most part it is the other way around, although I did once manage to teach a cat that I didn't appreciate dead birds.

The behaviour of cats can present us with many mysteries. The homing instincts of cats can sometimes compare quite favourably with that of the homing pigeon, for although the pigeon is obviously faster and can fly across seas, cats also have been known to negotiate hundreds of miles in order to return to their old homes. Nobody knows why or how.

They are clearly able to fend for themselves on the journey, having never lost the hunting instincts and skills, as has happened in the case of domestic dogs, where it only seems to manifest when a collection of stray dogs will revert to basic instincts, gang up into small packs and hunt, to many a farmer's cost, and often the life of such a dog, because the farmer is legally entitled to shoot it if it is worrying his stock.

Cats will sometimes present us with strange little quirks of behaviour for which we can find no rational explanation, although it can be quite obvious that the cat knows exactly what it is up to.

My friend Wendy knew a cat that lived eight homes up the road. When the folk were out, and only then, this cat would make its own social call, politely come through Wendy's cat flap and make good use of the comforts in her home, returning to its own when it somehow knew its folks were back. Wendy's friend from up the road was often mystified that Wendy knew when they had been out. The truth was discovered when these friends visited Wendy themselves for a social chat and cup of tea, for as they walked in the front door, the cat walked in at the back to a face to face confrontation! A good laugh was had by all, probably including the cat!

In this case the cat clearly did know what it was doing and why, but another incident concerning Wendy's own cat defies human explanation. She once came across Smokey sitting contentedly by his feeding bowl – watching a mouse nibbling his dinner! The mouse scampered off at the human approach and the cat didn't even bother to chase it. Was this simply an unlikely friendship? – or had the mouse exercised some kind of hypnotic power over the cat? That explanation would more likely fit the other way around.

Humans often have unlikely friends, usually with their own kind, but sometimes with a different species, such as a snake or fox, so why shouldn't animals themselves have unlikely friends and acquaintances. This incident suggests that they do, and there are in fact countless such situations around the world.

Perhaps the behaviour of animals is nearer to our own than we realise. Maybe cats are not quite so remote as we believe, perhaps in their wisdom they are just not letting on, somehow knowing the value of a mystery to the human race, because it is quite obvious that cats really do know a thing or two, especially about their "owners". Perhaps we could learn a thing or two from our feline companions.

PUSSYCAT, PUSSYCAT

(Where Have You Been?)

Have you seen a little cat
    Anywhere about?
I saw her here this morning
    Of that I have no doubt.

She was playing with a butterfly,
    Although she would not hurt it,
Just touch it with a gentle paw,
    And then she sits to watch it.

I've searched all through our cupboards,
    Peeped into our armchairs.
I've looked inside our motor car,
    To catch her unawares.

I've searched our neighbour's garden,
    Looked for paw prints on the ground,
In fact I've looked just everywhere,
    But no pussycat I found.

I've sorted out the garage,
    Rummaged out our garden shed.
Oh there you are – you naughty puss,
    You're curled up in my bed!

A PLACE IN THE WATER

Water – the lifeblood of the world, from trickling stream to mighty ocean and one of our most essential assets. We love it or grumble about it depending on it being the right amount – too much or too little – and whether or not it comes at the right time and in the right place. Too much can bring disaster to our prize roses or a whole nation. Too little and our vegetable plots shrivel and so can a nation. We often forget how dependent we are on water at the right time in the right place – we simply take it for granted in places where it flows freely.

There is other life however to whom it is even more important – the animal life that actually lives in water, the rivers, lakes and seas – these would die an even quicker death without water, and are very dependent on the way we use and treat our supplies – *their* supplies.

At the top of the water dependent scale, we have the whales and dolphins, the warm-blooded mammals of the oceans with a brain that is proportionally larger than any other animal.

We have exploited the whale for commercial purposes ever since man learned how to ride the seas in boats, until some became endangered species. Several organisations have worked extremely hard to protect these friendly animals of the sea; Greenpeace, The International Fund for Animal Welfare and the Whale and Dolphin Conservation Society can all claim a rightful share in protecting them and getting legislation changed on an international scale, that has halted the damage inflicted by man. But *still* there are commercial interests that find loopholes in the law through which they can squeeze, which emphasizes the fact that people of compassion cannot afford to sit back in congratulatory mood. There always seems to be someone somewhere ready to negate the good that has been done, to flout the law for their own gain, indicating a very low level of spirituality. When the seas no longer run red with the blood of the whale, we can all hold our heads a little higher.

Dolphins seem to come into a slightly different category of our emotions and interest. We actually have genuine affection for them, and they appear to reciprocate this feeling. There are hundreds of stories throughout history of them helping sailors in distress. There are even more of friendly dolphins metaphorically attaching themselves to ships for awhile, cavorting around without a sign of fear, and apparently enjoying the attention they evoke. They seem to actually enjoy human company and we certainly enjoy theirs.

I have some inner feeling that dolphins are more important to us than we realise. Something about them makes them a symbolic challenge to our own intelligence and spirituality. They only seem to try and be friends. They trust us, strange animals of the seas that they are, they appear to know a thing or two that we don't, and I feel that we betray them at our peril, for in doing so we would reveal an insensitivity that would be our eventual undoing. Somewhere, deep down inside, so many people know this, that dolphins have in the past been spared the wholesale commercial slaughter of the whales. More recently dolphins have become the unintentional victims of modern fishing methods for tuna and other fish. Being mammals, they will of course drown if held under water, thus, caught in the huge tuna nets, they have become the victims of commercial greed – the uncaring, unthinking elements of mankind who are willing to exploit anything and everything for monetary gain.

On a smaller scale we have the live capture of dolphins and even whales, for the amusement of human onlookers in dolphinaria. Surely no-one who has witnessed the joyful freedom of these animals in the vast expanses of the sea, can condone the limitations of their captivity – just for the amusement of humans – would *we* be prepared to sacrifice our own freedom to amuse *them*? I doubt it, so where is our superiority and compassion here?

Quite apart from the actual cruelty and exploitation of the animals of the sea, mankind has been polluting and overfishing it for a very long time. In my early years there was a saying that there were more fish in the sea than ever came out of it, which is a very false premise in 1991, which demonstrates how greedily we exploit our own essential assets. Modern fishing methods, larger ships, huge nets with smaller mesh all contribute to the catastrophe. Misinformed management about such things as fishing quotas can mean dead fish being thrown back into the sea, where only the gulls can benefit and the fish has died in vain. Other rules allow catches to be used simply as fertilizer for our landlocked soil instead of direct use as food. Vegetarians would certainly see the stupidity of such mismanagement, and it helps to make the point that if more people would follow vegetarian principles, most of these problems would gradually disappear.

The destruction of the wildlife of the seas by cruelty and killing is accelerated by the pollution we deliberately or carelessly spill into it, from radioactive waste to oil and dangerous chemicals, from sewage to mercury and all stops in between. Some people seem to think that anything we don't want can be dumped into the sea, but one only has to watch an incoming tide bringing ashore the visible flotsam and jetsam to realise that the invisible wastes can come back to us that way as well. Meanwhile it has been poisoning the seas and its inhabitants, some of which is being caught for human consumption, while the seals and their wide-eyed fluffy pups will be dying of pollution if they escape the knife and truncheon of the seal fur trade. Much hard work has been done, and earned legislation towards protection for all these animals of the seas, and if some folk complain they are eating the fish we need, let us not forget that *they* were there first, and we cannot expect *them* to adopt vegetarian eating habits, their digestive systems were not designed for it – but ours were, so we could!

If we think we are making a giant dustbin of our seas, we must also accept that we are also destroying our rivers, lakes and other wetlands. Will we *never* learn?

Our heritage of rivers, canals and lakes is of such vital importance the world over, that it is almost beyond comprehension that they are so neglected and misused. Waterfowl and waders depend on them in a variety of different ways, but especially for food and during migration. Some domestic and farm animals drink from the rivers, whilst some of our wild animals not only drink from them but actually live in them as well, otters for example, and for these our polluted rivers are lethal and in the end the pollution reaches the human consumer. That beautiful book about Tarka the otter was based on the river Torridge in North Devon. That river, at the time of writing is one of the worst polluted rivers in our country and the otters have gone, only a newly developed nature trail remains as a memorial to a memorable book and beautiful animal – The Tarka Trail – that is, until someone can permanently clean the the river fit for otters to live in, and the local people care enough about their river to keep it that way, a challenge for people who care.

The first sign of river or lake pollution is often supplied by fish. The river authorities make gallant efforts to keep their charges in good order, but industry and modern farming methods are unfortunately often the cause of the pollution that brings the fish floating, dead and unsightly to the surface, the river plants suffering the same fate. Volunteers frequently work hard to overcome the damage, thus demonstrating their own higher spirituality without perhaps realising it. But often it is only to endure a repeat performance of the pollution.

Our rivers and lakes not only give us all much pleasure, they are the homes of wildlife that is part of the essential natural chain of all life, for everything in this world is dependent on something else, frequently on *many* other aspects of existence. If we complain that herons eat our river fish, it is the price we pay for the pleasure of seeing these birds in patient action, so quietly setting about the daily business of living – just as we have to do, but they are in sharp contrast to the human rush to save a few minutes of time that we then don't know how to use anyway. If we don't look after the fish and insect life of the rivers, we say goodbye to the beautiful kingfisher and all other river life. If we fail to accept that we must share our waterways and seas with the bird and animal life of our world and look after them properly, we are failing both them and ourselves by our own stupidity, for water is such an essential commodity for us all – but let us not forget, the animals were there first, they are entitled to a place in the water.

If I should cry
Please weep for me,
If I should sigh,
Please set me free
From all the horrors
Of the sea.

THE BIRD TABLE OR CHALLENGE MR. SQUIRREL

In my family, feeding our garden birds has been a regular habit for as long as I can remember. Bird tables and nestboxes have been part of our garden furniture since I was about five years old. But they became of much greater significance when a very dear cousin passed to Spirit.

Winnie had nursed her father and then her husband through terminal illnesses, and during those times had kept them amused and interested by the simple act of feeding the garden birds, keeping a continuous supply of food to attract an equally continuous supply of birds for the benefit of her patients. She continued the practice after both father and husband had left their earthly lives behind, until she too succumbed to illness to join them. Her last words were to her good friend and neighbour – "Please feed my birds for me".

Edith and I decided that wherever we were, we would always keep in touch with each other on the anniversary of Winnie's passing and that our memorial to her would be to feed the birds daily. Thus our bird tables are modest shrines to a lovely gentle soul, and the birds in our respective gardens are very appreciative of this idea. So much so in fact, that they in their turn reward us well in entertainment, just as their predecessors did over twenty years ago.

There is however another angle to bird tables, that can be a pleasure or a nuisance, depending on which way you look at it. The added dimension is provided in some gardens by Mr. Squirrel, that jolly acrobatic opportunist of woodlands that has discovered the easy pickings of our garden bird tables. If ever an animal proved its ability to think and reason for itself, the squirrel has surely made its point.

Our own challenge with Mr. Squirrel occurred when we lived near Christchurch in Dorset. Our nut holder hung on a bracket attached to the fence until the squirrel made short work of the contents, one at a time at first, and then by removing the base, allowing the entire contents to fall to the ground. He (or she) was overwhelmed by the sudden glut of food and it was amusing to watch his indecision as to which nut to pick up next. We temporarily solved the problem for both squirrel and ourselves by hanging the container on the whirlygig clothes line arms. Within a few hours he was running up the pole and along the arms of the apparatus to the nuts. I moved them along to the centre of the outside length of line – he solved the problem within about three minutes by running along the line upside-down. My next move in this game of squirrel chess was to lightly grease the centre pole with an edible oil, (not wishing to harm my friendly opponent). This baffled my friend for a whole day, as he jumped on to the pole and promptly slid down again. The look on his face as he studied the situation, sniffed at the pole, examined his paws and tried yet again, was a study in itself. By the next morning he had solved the problem. He decided to leap from a nearby shed on to the whirlygig – a matter of about five feet – run along the arms of the apparatus to the nuts.

The challenge was finally settled when we bought from the Royal Society for the Protection of Birds, a nut cage that hung within another cage. The birds could reach the nuts, Mr. Squirrel could not. I felt so sorry for him that I gave him a daily ration of nuts in their shells as compensation and in appreciation of the entertainment he had given us. He in his turn 'rewarded' us by the antics of picking up each nut, stuffing several in his mouth and racing off across the garage with them. We later discovered what he was doing with them when we found several peanut plants growing in the garden! If we had stayed in that house, we might have had our own groundnut scheme eventually, thanks to Mr. Squirrel and his charming, aggravating ways. I must admit I enjoyed the challenge and missed him when we left. I wonder if he missed me too, the new occupants promised to feed him, but I have a feeling that it wasn't quite the same for him, because I remember so well his cheeky face and outstretched paws as he took the nuts from my hand – I'm not sure he would have trusted someone else in quite the same way.

In retrospect, my challenge with Mr. Squirrel pin points the problem of how far we should go in providing sustenance for our wild animals and birds. Could we be making them too dependent upon us?

Some thought about this aspect of conservation makes us realise that most of the problems for our wild life are man-made in one way or another, it must therefore be our prerogative and even duty to do the best we can to alleviate those problems. Through the years we have interfered with nature to such an extent, upset the balance in so many ways and places that we are now in danger of losing the very ingredients that we have used and mismanaged so much in the past. At last we are realizing our dependence on those things of nature that we need to survive ourselves.

Our modest challenge with the squirrel and the bird table is a case in point. Grey squirrels were not natives of Britain, but imported from America – by man. Next, we reduce the habitat and food sources by clearing woodlands and hedges, and spreading our towns, villages and cities over more and more of the countryside that is the natural home for our wildlife. With food supplies and home sites dwindling, the animals do exactly the same as the human does, move on to conditions that are easier for them. In the process of this, the grey squirrel has largely taken over from our native red squirrel which is now becoming increasingly rare, whilst the grey has survived so well that in some places they are now being shot as vermin because of over-population. A classic case of the balance of nature being upset by the activities of mankind, who then doesn't know how to deal with the resulting problems without killing. 'Thou shalt not kill' we are told, which merely leaves us with further problems of mankind's own making, as opinions vary, standards conflict with one another, and wildlife continues to die or fade away.

However, it is not all gloom and doom. On the contrary, the awareness that has increased so much in recent years of our past mistakes and our need to rectify them, is a very positive step forward.

In the realization that mankind is to blame for the sickness of the earth and all that is therein, it becomes obvious that he is morally bound to bring about the cures. The past cannot be undone, progress must be by looking forward, with only the lessons of the past to guide the treatment. In treating the patient we cannot expect to restore all the old conditions. In some cases it may not be even the best thing anyway for the future conditions. Having learnt those lessons from past mistakes, we can now go ahead to restore the balance of nature, with those mistakes as guidelines, towards a new and better world for all. Casualties there will be on the way, but each will play its own small part, nothing need ever die in vain, it is for us to feed the world the best things in life with spirituality in mind, as a memorial to those who lived and died, those who have worked and tried upon this earthplane for a little while – the bird table of life.

My own bird table rewards me amply, as the blue, coal and great tits peck happily away at the nuts we supply – this time squirrel free so far.

They hop and pop cheekily around, squabble amongst themselves at times, as their human counterparts will do. They build their homes, raise their young and introduce them to our bird table – tiny bundles of fluffy feathers, knowing, or being taught just what to do. They prey upon their parents' protective instincts, pretending they cannot hang on a nut cage to feed, when they, I and their mums and dads know perfectly well they can, but its a jolly good way of getting attention and easy food – shades of human children! Whilst there is so much difference between many worldly things, it is yet amazing how much there is the same. Only people sometimes spoil the view.

Our memorial bird table continues to play its own small part in conservation, supplying regularly (most important) sustenance for our tiny acrobats – mini miracles of life. We who serve at table are part of those miracles, part of the balance of nature that brings prosperity to the soul, the smiles and tears, the wonder of creation. Thank you Mr. Squirrel for helping with the lesson.

HALF AN INCH TO SIX TONS

People have tamed and domesticated animals since time immemorial. There is an enormous variety of animals that has developed alongside human owners and equally varying reasons why this is so. This applies even today as different types of people choose to be involved with different members of the animal kingdom. Sometimes the lure of material profit enters into the decisions – apart from liking a certain breed of cat or dog, breeding from them or showing them can be profitable. People who fancy keeping birds can do the same thing. In years gone by silk worms fulfilled a similar purpose.

Silk worms have rather fallen out of favour in western countries, and were never so established as they were in China, where the practice began and the secrets of silk production were so jealously guarded a few thousand years ago, that death was the punishment for revealing them abroad. Thankfully, although breeders of animal life still guard their own pet secrets of success, punishment for disloyalty in this respect is virtually non-existent. Only the wrath of the owner remains as a pale reflection of outdated retribution, with death only for the silk worm.

Breeders of all kinds of birds, animals and insects invariably seek to 'improve' their strains, often to the detriment of some other aspect of the animal, by interbreeding in attempts to enhance certain aspects. This interference with nature is another example of mankind's egoistical attitude towards animals. The results manifest in some inherent weakness appearing after a while. In the case of cats and dogs it can be anything from structural weaknesses to temperament changes. Unnatural practices such as tail docking and the fancy clipping of fur in certain breeds of dog are today merely a matter of fashion on the part of the owners, although there were once sound reasons for them. Other breeds are often bred with unnaturally long coats that delight the owners and judges at shows, but are a nuisance to the dog, thus we manipulate the animals in our care to our own advantage rather than theirs.

Horses too have grown almost out of recognition from their wild ancestors. From those wild herds man has developed every strain in use today, from the child's riding pony to the swiftest racehorse and majestic heavy horse of the ploughed field and brewer's dray. Here, man does not seem to have done the same damage that has been inflicted on the world of dogs and cats. Perhaps sheer proud strength stood the horse in good stead. In their case, we even admit now to the folly of tail docking, so perhaps there is yet hope that this practice will soon be outlawed for dogs as well, as mankind moves slowly towards greater kindness for his animals.

Many pets inevitably have to be kept in cages, often too small, frequently not properly cleaned. But children often learn their first lessons in kindness from gerbils, hamsters and guinea pigs. They can also find introduction to the facts of life and death in a perfectly natural way that they can readily understand, a method that is far superior to cold impersonal lessons from books and school teachers or stumbling half truths from embarrassed parents. These small pets serve us well and deserve better conditions than many have to endure. Early lessons in personal responsibility can be acquired through these little animals. Regular feeding, watering and cleaning are easy tasks for children to perform, and it is a pity so many parents allow this sense of responsibility to wane and take on the tasks of caring themselves, while the children move on to new interests – a great opportunity to learn about life is then lost.

Children also learn other essential facts from their pets besides the practical ones. By cuddling a soft furry rabbit they learn the importance of touch and demonstrating affection. They learn about compassion and sharing, and any hidden dangers associated with their pets. The value of a small pet to a child can hardly be overestimated.

Some people choose to keep exotic or unusual pets that can provide a very wide range of interest. Most people neither like nor understand snakes, possibly a legacy from early bible teachings about serpents, complemented later by mysticism in Eastern countries with such practices as snake charming for example. One result of this choice of a pet can therefore be a reputation for the owner to be rather weird, simply because he (it is usually a he) does not conform to the usual pattern of animal keepers. The poor reputation of the snake is quite unfounded – it is not even cold and slimy as so many people believe. However, it is not really an ideal pet from the point of view of the snake. It has to be kept caged in some way, and its natural wandering habits of the wild are curtailed to an unacceptable extreme. They can also grow very large, a python may reach thirty feet. Some snakes need to be fed live food, and this fact means that the owner must sacrifice some other animal in order to feed his snake. This can be an emotive situation, because of course it is arguable that some animals have to die to feed others in the wild, and our own pet dogs and cats are fed meat that once lived. I do not feel that these are valid points, because all animal life in the wild is able to take its fair chance with predators, and every one is endowed with its own protective system of life – that is the wisdom of nature. If we drop a live mouse into the limited area of a snake's vivarium, the mouse has no such chance, it has been sentenced to death by the snake's human owner, and not given its natural chances of escape. In the case of feeding our own pets it doesn't seem quite the same thing to feed a pet from meat already killed, as to set out to feed it live food which it must kill for itself. There are people who actually feed their dogs on vegetarian food and they seem to thrive well enough on this. Dogs have perhaps come so far away from their wild conditions that they are able to adapt in spite of their stomachs being designed to digest meat. Cats on the other hand do not so easily respond to this kind of interference in the pattern of their lives and most vets would advise against such a change. Most cats would probably rectify the situation themselves by going out to catch some food on their own account. In this imperfect world there are few perfect solutions to these or any other problems. We can only do our best according to our own consciences.

Exotic birds and animals have always had an appeal for some people. The desire to possess something different or better than other people is an inherent weakness that many people find hard to overcome. The trait is expressed in many ways apart from the keeping or choice of a pet animal. It reveals itself in clothes, cars, houses, boats and general paraphernalia, but as these are inanimate objects no harm is done apart from possibly having an adverse effect on the nature of the owners. When the trait includes animals a different situation arises.

Rescuing a lioness and keeping her in loving care was one thing (Joy Adamson and Elsa the lioness) but deliberately taking on a leopard cub that has no problems for instance, purely to keep it as a pet and take it out on a lead is quite another matter. The cat family does not respond to such limitations, and the ones that are still so near to their wild state as a leopard should never be so humiliated. It is bad enough to see them pacing a cage in a zoo, but the totally unnatural environment of a human's luxury lounge must be an ego trip on the part of the owner.

Exotic birds probably suffer even more. Adult specimens caught in the wild are transported all over the world and only a few survive the privations of capture and journey. If they do survive they are sentenced to a life of imprisonment, without even committing a crime to merit such treatment. This practice is vastly different from the breeding of birds in captivity so that they have never known any other way of life. If smaller birds are then kept in good sized aviaries they can enjoy a measure of freedom and complete protection. Larger birds such as parrots can be kept on special stands with the freedom to properly stretch their wings, with the opportunity to fly if they wish, or at least enjoy a reasonable amount of unrestricted movement. Birds such as parrots, budgerigars and canaries can give lonely people a great deal of comfort and companionship without any real stress to the birds and thereby give a service to mankind. It only seems a pity that such problems as loneliness arise for the human owners in the first place, creating such a need, but as this situation is unlikely to diminish we must be thankful for the birds that help to overcome these sad situations.

There is pressure at the time of writing to outlaw the capture and transport of wild birds, but like so many other sad situations the laws would not be necessary if people did not create these bad circumstances in the first place. In this case, people should refrain from buying such birds as these. With the demand gone, so would the profit of capturing them. It's as simple as that.

Our wild birds too have served man well, even though they sometimes make a modest charge for their efforts. The bullfinch receives much abuse for the destruction of buds that we had hopes of turning into fruit, but on the other hand this bird also takes the grubs for breakfast that would have spoilt our fruit in any case. The golden eagle may fly off with an occasional lamb to the fury of the shepherd and certainly the distress of the lamb and its mother, but frequently it is a sickly lamb whose death has only been hastened, meanwhile the eagle has also cleared away unsightly carrion that could cause disease for other animals. It all eventually returns to that balance of nature that mankind is so carelessly destroying in pursuance of his own greed. He has yet to learn to share.

The dog has undoubtedly given a wider range of service to the human race than any other animal. Mankind has been able to manipulate and train its many natural skills and instincts to his own advantage, and it has proved to be a willing pupil. It is born with a strong pack loyalty and often an individual loyalty within the pack. If domesticated dogs have now come to regard human families as their packs, it is certainly to our advantage.

Apart from their obvious value to us as pets, dogs give us unstinting loyalty and service for merely the price of their keep.

Any affection we give them is a well earned entitlement rather than a conditional reward. The story probably began with guarding and hunting, when catching animals for food was a necessity rather than the 'sport' and social event it is today. Man soon learned to use dogs for guarding sheep from predators and his own home from molestation. It was a short step to promote the dogs from merely guarding the sheep to controlling them. Thus we have our well trained and knowledgeable sheepdogs and to a lesser extent, cattle dogs on our farms. Since then, the dogs' other qualities and ability to learn has enabled us to train them to guide the blind, hear on behalf of the deaf, rescue people that are lost on mountains and places of the wild. Some dogs specialize in some of these activities. The St. Bernard is famous for its mountain work, while the lesser known Newfoundland is an expert at rescue from watery graves. Thousands of people were found and saved from bombed buildings during World War II through the work of the rescue dogs that became widely used. The ability was accidentally discovered by an Air Raid Warden who was in the habit of taking his Wire Hair Terrier along to the Warden's Post when he was on duty. After a raid this dog would accompany her owner to the scene of the destruction and begin frantically digging where people were buried, thus saving precious time in the search. So enthusiastically did Beauty dig, that she had to be provided with purpose-made boots to protect her bleeding paws. The value of her efforts was recognised and many dogs were successfully trained to indicate without damage to their own feet.

This same instinct has been used for tracking down drugs and explosives, finding clues and bodies in murder hunts and searching for lost people. This has been a recognised skill of Bloodhounds for many years, but other breeds are now more commonly used, the Alsatian German Shepherd dog being particularly versatile as a friend of man, unless of course it is on guard duty, in which case it is best to be on the right side of its idea of law and order! A dog will sacrifice its life to protect its owner – I wonder how many owners would do the same for their dogs?

Butterflies do not really come into the category of pets, but the breeding of butterflies is an absorbing interest that has the merit of conservation because so many of the species are fast disappearing as a result of the selfish activities of mankind. While there are a few people who have the interest, space and money to follow this absorbing hobby, we stand a chance of saving at least some of these beautiful creatures. Perhaps the entomologist of today can keep things going for long enough for the human race to come to its senses and protect the natural environments of the butterfly along with that of the tiger, polar bear and elephant.

The elephant, although it is hardly everyone's idea of a pet, has given great service to the human race for a very long time. This gentle giant of warmer climes has played a valuable part in the lives and cultures of the people in the regions of its natural habitat. The rich and poor reaped advantageously from the power and kindly nature of this huge animal of forests and plains. Its ability to root up trees is a natural part of its own existence, and although this did a lot of damage it was also put to good use once the animal was tamed. It could carry those trees using its own trunk, pull enormous loads and provide transport for the menial or pomp and circumstance of religious ceremony. It became a status symbol, the more elephants that were owned, the richer and higher on the social scale. Yet the elephant has received poor recompense from the human race for its services. Pampered by the rich in its native India it may have been, but this is not the elephant's style, it is majestic enough in its own right, it seems out of place in ceremonial fancy dress, and is even more incongruous as a circus performer in the West. The elephant has great intelligence and the strength to wreak havoc in any religious festival or circus ring, but it doesn't, it patiently continues to serve mankind in his foolish ways. In return for all this, the animal has been hunted almost to extinction for the sake of its ivory tusks. Such things as doorstops have been made from its feet, sold and bought as gruesome souvenirs. If a female with calf is killed, the baby may be left to be starved of food, comfort and care, or perhaps be killed itself. The World Wildlife Fund and World Society for the Protection of Animals have done a great deal to alleviate all these difficulties and many more besides, in all parts of the world as their names indicate, but the more we think about such things, the more we realise that some sections of the human race fall far short of the animals over whom they have power, but in the case of the elephant it has from time immemorial had the greater strength, yet rarely used it against its own tormentors. It is a puzzle that it should retain its patience and integrity against such provocation.

All life on earth is dependent in some way on other earthly life, and in its turn contributes to others. This is the balance of nature, the circle of all living. Animals, great and small, play their part by instinct or an inner knowledge that we do not yet understand. People have the gift of choice as to how, what, when and where they give and take, and misuse the gift at great cost, for the balance of nature is the essential component to sustain life on earth.

Through these glimpses of animal life and human living, from the tiny to the great of both worlds, we can begin to see the necessity for mankind to mend its ways and adjust its thinking. We have on our hands the modern version of that age-old battle between good and evil. Human beings have the knowledge and power to put things right, but have we got amongst us enough spirituality? Perhaps a closer look at the butterfly and elephant will help us back on to the right tracks, for in these things we find our own creation.

THE ELEPHANT AND THE EAGLE!

Said the eagle to the elephant,
Whatever will you do
When your time has come for heaven?
Your weight will preclude you!

My wings will reach the shining stars,
But you surely will be grounded,
Oh no, the elephant replied,
Your theory is unfounded.

For while you shed warm blood for food,
I was feeding me on grass,
No pain inflicted for *my* fill,
But you killed for your repast.

The eagle wept, he did not know
Such kindly food was there,
But the elephant, he smiled his last –
And flew to heaven on a prayer!

A PLACE IN HEAVEN

All animal life has its own part to play in earthly life, and although it is obvious that human beings have their own important role in the worldly scheme of things, it is not always appreciated that the animal kingdom is just as important in creating the balance of nature, and that both aspects of life also play their specific parts in spiritual life after so-called death.

Many people find it difficult to accept this continued existence for the human species, and even more stumble at the thought of animal survival. Yet all through the history of mankind there has been a basic belief in survival after earthly life. Every religion in the world teaches it in some form or other, yet still the human mind can be reluctant to accept it as a very real and true fact.

The main stumbling block is proof. Through aeons of time, proof of survival has been manifest, but most religions demand blind faith, and many people who wish to exercise the prerogative of thinking for themselves cannot accept such a system. But through those years, mankind has also been indoctrinated to believe it wrong to commune with those who have passed on to a greater world, thereby precluding proof. The shackles of these indoctrinations are hard to shake off, and even harder when the subject of animal survival comes to the fore.

In our own country, the Christian religion is the prominent spiritual guideline, and this is the one with ample evidence of spirit communication and survival after death in its own Bible and New Testament, so one has to ask why there is so much doubt.

Many books and spirit communications have studied the subject and given answers that are acceptable and even irrefutable, so that it is not part of our task to go into it again here, it is sufficient to observe that the evidence is there for those who wish to find it, and that it is only the interpretation over hundreds of years that has misled and cast doubt. Many earthly teachers must obviously take much of the blame for the misunderstandings, and it is not our task to stir still further the confusions that have arisen as a result of these misinterpretations. Our concern is to further the cause of Spirit by helping people to understand that they may go forward in their own knowledge and development, and in this book in particular, they may find some of that knowledge through the animal kingdom and thereby also further the cause of the animals themselves.

With this in view, I will write of some of the evidence for animal survival that has come my way. In doing so, it is worthy of note, that if animals survive the earthly state we call death, then it is obvious that the human spirit also survives it. Usually these two facts are placed in opposite positions, the human survival presenting animal survival as a possibility. Here we concentrate upon the animal aspect, believing that this will automatically state the case for the peoples of the whole world.

I must apologise to those readers who have read our last book *Memory Rings The Bells*, for some of the following incidents appear therein but are certainly worthy of mention here for new reader friends, because they prove animal survival so well.

A well-known London Medium, Jessie Nason, once gave me superb evidence of the survival of my German Shepherd dog Judy, some of whose other achievements appear elsewhere in this book. Jessie not only described the dog accurately, but also reminded me of one of her little fun tricks, swinging her tail-end round as she passed by, knocking me in the back of my knee. Her mischievous face and gaily wagging tail as she paused to look at me, were evidence enough of her playful intention. Jessie explained that Judy still did this sometimes to draw my attention. I realised then that the slight bump I sometimes felt behind the knee was in fact my dear old dog still playing games – it was not after all my imagination playing tricks as I had thought.

Jessie Nason and I had never met before and knew nothing about each other, so that her further remarks provided still more evidence for animal survival of death. She mentioned seeing literally hundreds of pets of all kinds that were making their presence known at the time, because I had given them and their owners some special service. Jessie could not have known that I worked for the People's Dispensary for Sick Animals for twenty years, and that a major part of my job had been to arrange for burial or cremation of the earthly remains of those pets.

A cat once gave me good survival evidence and a slight shock at the same time. As I opened the door of a New Forest cottage, where my husband Ken had lived happily with his first wife Myrtle, a black and white cat dashed past me and into the garden. As the cottage was at the time only housing furniture, I was naturally a bit startled, and looked out into the garden to see where it had gone. It was nowhere to be seen. On enquiring of Ken if they had ever had a black and white cat, his confirmation was pretty reliable evidence, as this was something I did not previously know. As the cat and I had never been acquainted, there was of course no reason for it to appear to me. But it is a well-known fact that cats frequently attach themselves more to their home than to people, but in any case the cat's owner Ken, was only a few yards away, a fact which may well have helped puss to materialise – before my very eyes!

A friend once asked me to visit another friend of hers, who was concerned about one or two strange happenings in her home. I specifically asked the lady not to give me any details, but simply allow me to walk around the house to see what I could detect. Having gone through all the downstairs rooms, I finally came to a bedroom where I felt there was a kindly and elderly gentleman, although I could not see him. The lady confirmed that the room had been her father's, and that my description fitted him. I was then able to describe a dog which I *could* see, and the animal was recognised as one that had belonged to her father. Once the lady knew the cause of the strange happenings, she was happy to know that her father came back sometimes and particularly pleased that he still had his much loved pet dog with him, and was now contented, because that was the strong impression being conveyed to me. In this case there was presumably insufficient power for the gentleman to actually appear himself, and he might in any case have not realised that he could do so. The dog would have no such inhibitions, and would simply have done what came naturally, and in the process giving much added evidence for the daughter of his master – a service of a very different kind to the usual help we receive from pets.

During clairvoyance at Christchurch Spiritualist church on one occasion, the Medium came to me with the name of Joe, at which I shook my head while my mind searched for someone of that name. The Medium then corrected and said, "Sorry, its not Joe, its Joey, and its the name of a budgerigar and a very nice lady is asking me to tell you she has him with her, and thanks you for your help". This I could most certainly accept. The owner was my much loved cousin Winnie, the budgerigar belonged to her, and was one of the pets I had buried in the P.D.S.A. cemetery. My cousin had loved her pet so much, obviously still did, and between them they provided some simple but sound evidence of their survival of earthly death.

During the communications for our second book "I'm Jane", this little girl in Spirit, made us all very much aware of the pet animals around her and described in some detail her life there with them. She also told of a fox with whom she became friendly, and it seemed that it no longer displayed the less likeable habits that we on earth attribute to foxes. Presumably they were no longer necessary, which creates a pleasing and peaceful picture of the Spirit World to which we can all look forward. If that sly old Reynard of our childhood story books can survive and become a peaceful and happy citizen of the Spirit World, then surely so can we, and our own pets along with us!

Those people who truly love their pets, can obviously take comfort in the knowledge of their survival after death. I hope that many who read these words will now realise that those same pets can return and make their presence felt to their owners still on the earthplane. When they do, please do not ignore them, you wouldn't do so when they were on earth, and you could give them the same joy that you gave them then by acknowledging their presence in Spirit. It is only a matter of being conscious of those funny little habits they always had previously on earth but now in their place in heaven – just a different dimension – only a thought away.

HIS SPECIAL PLACE

What's that bumping in the kitchen?
  That thumping on the floor?
Oh its only Fido scratching,
  Just like he did before –
Before he slipped from earthly life
  Through doggie heaven's door.

Now his days are fun and games,
  Life without a care,
My father has his company,
  And *he's* got Dad's armchair!
It happened when they were on earth,
  So I'm sure it happens there.

But Fido comes to see me still,
  I know when he's around,
He thumps the floor with his scratching leg,
  Tail wagging I'll be bound.
I cannot see him now of course,
  But I *know* that familiar sound!

A PLACE IN THE FOREST

Air – just about everything in the world needs it, even water must have air to oxygenate it, and most of all we need that air to be pure to sustain healthy life. So why on earth are we so busily polluting it, gradually destroying every link in the life chain?

But all is not lost – trees can help us to restore the balance, both physically and spiritually. Trees can absorb impurities in the air and turn it into life giving oxygen, but we do need a lot of them. Unfortunately, mankind in his foolishness and often ignorance, has been destroying the trees faster than they have been replaced or grown.

In the early days of man's evolution, this knowledge was too far advanced for him – he just did not know the catastrophe he was setting in motion – but we know now and have done so for many years, a fact that prompted the organisation known as The Men Of The Trees around seventy years ago, and their world-wide reafforestation plans.

The problem is on a world-wide scale, the effects are also felt by the whole world. The cure must therefore involve every nation, all the people. World-wide understanding and co-operation is called for and immediate action.

Fortunately, many wise and sensitive minds have been alerted to this serious misuse of yet another natural asset, and their voices are at last being heard. We are now fully aware of the destructive acid rain that falls upon our woodlands and forests as a result of air pollution. With that awareness comes the responsibility of curing the air of this malady.

The wholesale destruction of trees for commercial purposes, at a greater rate than they are replaced, is unforgivable greed now that we know the folly of such action. The situation is serious enough here in Great Britain. In the rain forests abroad it is even more far reaching, where vast areas are being cleared, and local people and governments seem unwilling or unable to accept the facts of their destruction. Difficult as life may be for them at the present time, it will be infinitely worse as time goes on. So here again, drastic action is called for at once, and help given to people who have depended upon the felling of trees in the past. A new way of life has to be introduced, lest their livelihood be lost altogether.

These are the aspects of trees and forests that directly affect the people of the world. Where we are affected, so also are the animals, especially those that live in forests and woodlands – those animals and plants that directly depend on trees for food, shelter and breeding places.

Rare orchids and butterflies, leopards, chimpanzees and elephants are just a few examples of the forest wildlife that desperately needs our protection. Hundreds more, like birds of paradise and tigers, owls and woodpeckers will fade away – never to be seen again except in photographs unless we heed the warnings quickly.

Numerous species have either seriously declined or disappeared already because of the ravages we inflict on our forests and woodland areas the world over. In Great Britain we still have a number of birds and animals that are dependent on trees, and it becomes daily more urgent to protect them, not only for the animals but also for ourselves. To idly argue that we need the wood as timber or the space the trees occupy, only brings nearer the day when we are forced to do without them simply because the trees are no longer there. They will have disappeared along with the deer, owls and squirrels that depended on them for life.

Fortunately it is not yet too late, thousands of trees are being planted by nature conservancy organisations, charities and individual people, who are not only planting, but protecting trees as they grow. Some organisations are protecting birds, whilst others are concerned with insect or animal life, for others the objective is general conservancy for all, including the human race. All play a very worthwhile part towards the rescue of our forests and woods. People are making a point of planting trees in their own gardens. Not everyone can accommodate a stately oak, but many of us can find the space for something smaller, and each one is a contribution towards the whole. Trees are for everyone and everything, our very existence ultimately depends upon them.

Trees also have a less well known part to play in our lives, for apart from the practical earthly service that they give us, there are the spiritual and healing gifts that are delivered to us via the trees, aspects that are not so generally realised in our modern times, although many ancient civilisations were well aware of them.

With all our advance in technology, all our achievements and discoveries, we have almost lost sight of many simple and wonderful facts and one of these is the power of the trees.

Earlier peoples knew and understood these gifts to the world – the North American Indians for example were very knowledgeable in such matters and many of their beliefs and spiritual activities connected with trees are well documented. But modern man has allowed that knowledge to slide away – he believes he has discovered something better instead of in addition. Arrogant commercialism adds its quota of destructive thinking, and we find that much worthwhile knowledge is being lost.

But always there are the few who still *know* – the few who recognise simple truth and facts and preserve that knowledge for mankind to reinvestigate and resurrect. The power of the trees is one of these, and many people now realise that by simply walking among trees they find peace and upliftment in a world of speed and sorrow. Some are aware of the healing power they can receive by standing with their back against a well matured tree. Many would not believe this simple fact, but those who lift their minds beyond mundane earthly thinking – if only for a little while – and allow their own soul to accept the healing with simplicity and love, *know.* No scientific mind or exploration has yet discovered the reasons or causes of this healing power, and so mankind with his materialistic outlook finds it hard to accept the truth of it.

We make the mistake of thinking that nothing can be effective unless we know the reason, and this is partly the result of our natural curiosity. We were given this aspect of our minds for a very good reason – progress of the right kind, but when we use it for only material purposes, we not only misuse it but narrow our field of vision and lose the spiritual aspect that would serve us so well.

Of all the mysteries of our planet, this is one that we *can* rescue from extinction, for along with the animals, birds, flowers and people, it has a place in the forest, and it is for us to preserve and guard that essential habitat.

THE OWL

How wise you are to be so wise
   To hunt the silence of the night,
While human efforts only rise
   When dawn has turned the dark to light.

How beautiful your silent glide,
   The mystery your eyes bestow
With all the dignity and pride
   On we who watch you from below.

Your call that echoes through the night,
   Sends shivers through a weaker spine,
But we who love you, feel delight
   To hear the soothing notes sublime.

May you ever grace our night-time,
   May our woodlands shelter still
The wonder of your sleeping daytime,
   Your evening call to ever thrill.

A BIRD IN HAND

It was a hot sultry day, early in September, and I was lounging in my armchair reading, my feet on a stool, Daisy on my lap and Poppette stretched out in her favourite position – along my legs.

Only the soft lazy twittering of a bird in the bushes near the open patio door broke the silence of rising heat on this rural late summer day.

Suddenly, a young great tit flew through the open door and sat perkily on a large mop headed succulent plant that stands only eighteen inches inside the door, about two feet from the floor, propped on a rather elegant umbrella vase masquerading as a plant stand.

Our feathered friend piped a couple of birdie notes, peered about the room, examined the plant on which he sat, then with a farewell "twit" flew out of the doorway on his way to the garden shrubs.

The two Yorkies mustered enough energy to raise their heads and peer quizzically at the tiny feathered visitor, but uncharacteristically, they made no response to the intrusion, perhaps they were too lazy or too astounded by the sheer audacity of it all. Or maybe they understood the bird language, (which of course I did not!) and realized that any reaction on their part was a waste of energy on a hot day.

I kept wondering what saucy remarks had been tossed out by our blue and yellow caller. With all our knowledge, some of which seems pretty useless anyway, no scientist has yet cracked bird vocal language, only some of their body language and a few seasonal sounds that do suggest a specific purpose.

Come to think of it, I feel that our own baby great tit was perhaps just saying thank you, because we do feed and water the birds regularly and give what protection we can from marauding magpies and buzzards, although of course *they* have to eat too, and they give a good service to mankind by clearing up a few unsavoury sights on roads and country walks. I hope they will forgive me for preferring our nut-cracking blue and great tits, after all, we can't all be actors and actresses on the stage of life, someone has to work behind the scenes, sweep the stage and clear up after everybody else, but our cheeky little blue on-stage dancers tug the heartstrings every time.

It is amazing how much we can learn from the birds, and equally surprising how little we still know after many years of investigation. On the physical level, some progress has been made. We believe for instance that we have cracked some of the mysteries of migration, but we have not unravelled the puzzle of the sheer stamina and strength that must be required to travel the distances regularly undertaken, often in adverse conditions. How *do* they know exactly when to start their journeys? "Instinct" comes the pat reply, but wait a minute – what *is* this mysterious thing we call instinct? Where is it housed? How do the birds acquire it? How does it guide them? How does it prompt a date on which to take off for distant parts – perhaps thousands of miles away? Where is such stamina stored in small birds? How do young birds know where to go when they have never been before – they do not always fly with their older counterparts? It is easier to imagine a large bird such as a goose flying long distances, but the mind can boggle at the thought of swallows, swifts and their kind. So many questions to be answered, we don't even know how much we don't know!

The homing pigeon that has given much sporting pleasure to mankind for so many years, has also given great service. No-one will ever know the number of lives saved by homing pigeons in wartime conditions. Before our own knowledge of radio waves was discovered, it was common practice to release a pigeon with a message attached to its leg, to fly from the front line of battle to its own loft where the message was received and forwarded to its ultimate destination.

Even after the advent of radio, homing pigeons were able to give service to mankind. In the Second World War, Resistance Movements on the Continent were able to send messages to England via 'Pigeon Post' when technology with radio had become so advanced that interception was a possibility that would have made its use dangerous, and pigeons were the lesser risk. Men lost in a wilderness, air crews that had crash landed on either sea or land, were halfway to rescue if they had a pigeon with them, it didn't even have the risk of batteries running out! It did however run the risk of being shot, and some did indeed make the ultimate sacrifice. Others battled on though injured, seemingly inspired by an extra ration of the instinct to survive, which we all share with them to some degree. At least one such bird was

awarded the Dicken Medal for bravery (a P.D.S.A. award). A study of
the history of the Pigeon Service makes one wonder if an extra strength
was indeed given to them – by whom? It seems a possible case of
Spirit protecting human beings via pigeons. We can only marvel at
their homing instincts and be thankful for this strange phenomena, the
tenacity and courage of the pigeon. Its only a pigeon of course – only?
Most of us could learn much from it.

Those raucous noisy birds, the gulls, also give us food for thought.
The sheer strength and skill with which they weather a storm, fills us
with amazement as they swirl and dive across mountainous seas, and
then drop nonchalantly on to those white capped, churning waves. No
sign of fear or difficulty as they face the storm, riding from whitehorse
top to murky troughs. Most of us would blanch at the thought of
landing on a smooth park lake, let alone the massive oceans of the
world in angry mood.

Their grace and beauty as they fly is a joy to behold. We watch, and
borrow for a moment or two the sense of freedom they express in
gliding, soaring flight, and forgive the disadvantages they sometimes
bring to our rooftops, our man-made promenades, and even our heads
or hats if we are walking beneath their flight at the wrong moment! We
must accept the noise they make in seaside suburbia and not complain.
Like everything else it is a swings and roundabouts situation, that harsh
cry on the land is but music along a wild and rugged coast. They give
service in various ways, clearing up the nasty bits on rubbish dumps or
seashore, without even a charge on the rates. And if they do also eat
our fish – was it not their's in the first place?

Each morning during autumn and winter months, thousands of gulls
work their way up our valley from the river Torridge to some unknown
inland destination, and every evening they return. I watch them from
our hillside home as they swirl in aerial patterns – a moving cloud of
silver, rising, diving, turning with one accord, as if one master mind
directs them – a sergeant major gull that shouts the order for them all
to follow with parade ground precision. They land in a field for a few
moments, in imitation of a drift of snow, then rise again, turn and soar
in unison and majesty, landing in the next field, only to rise again and
proceed up the valley field by field, perhaps·to follow a plough or find
a handy rubbish dump.

This little miracle never fails to fascinate me and confound my
limited knowledge. It makes me realise how little we really know

about the birds. We have used them for sport, food and decoration. We have kept them as pets, used them as bait to catch other birds or animals, kept aerodromes safe from starlings with them. We have made sanctuaries for them and at the same time destroyed their habitat. We have fed them yet taken away their natural food sources. We have protected them, poisoned and shot them and covered them in killing oil. We have listened and marvelled at their song and grumbled at the noise they make. We have learnt our own clumsy flying from the grace and aerodynamics of the birds. We have bred them in captivity for our own uses and reintroduced threatened species to the wild, having ourselves been the cause of the threat. We are cruel to them and often kind. We have admired them, loved and hated them. No wonder we know so little about them, we don't even seem to know what we do, or what we want to do about the birds. We just have to accept that in many ways they are still a mystery. They learn from us even as we learn from them, as anyone who feeds their garden birds regularly will know.

Birds sometimes hit our windows and lie unconscious on the ground. This is the moment when I can really help, first checking that wings, legs and neck are intact while the enforced sleep keeps them relaxed. If there is no damage, I then hold the bird between my warm hands until I feel it stir, having asked my healing friends to please give a hand of their own to help. Next I take a peep at the bird's head to see if the eyes are open, moving and responding. A little more time in hand until the movement increases, then I find a sheltered hiding place in the garden and gently place the patient there, making sure it doesn't flip over on its back. If it does, it must be held in the hands a little longer. We now keep a small recovery box handy for this recuperation time, keeping our patient safe from predators but free to go when it is ready. We have recently reduced these casualties by hanging roundels in the windows that usually cause the problem.

A bird in hand certainly stirs one's consciousness of their wonder yet vulnerability. A young owl, victim of a road accident, nursed back to health and perching on one's hand, brings with it a knowledge of the power we have over birds, and the owl brings too the realization of our own humility, as it perches there, trusting, wide-eyed and blinking in the daylight. It is so soft to the touch and will allow you to stroke it. It is so small, only thick feathers giving it a larger appearance. It makes one aware suddenly of a partnership, just for a few moments mankind and bird are one, part of each other's existence. Would that it could always be so. But we have to be content with learning from them and doing our rather inadequate best to conserve their kind, a humble but glorious purpose in life, as our minds fly with them high above restrictive earth.

Birds are part of our heritage and we are part of theirs, and so we must learn to live together, sharing this planet with all its wonders and difficulties. We can make the world a wonderful place for all the life that shares it, or we can destroy it with our ignorance and greed. Only mankind of earth's inhabitants wields this power, and so it is entirely up to us to guard these blessings, for without them we are all lost anyway, and will have much for which to answer in the life that comes after our earthly existence has faded and gone. It is for us here and now to preserve the wonders of the earth not only for ourselves but for the generations to come – and our feathered friends.

The beauty and grace of the birds, their freedom and knowledge are sources of inspiration for those who are in tune with nature. With them our minds can fly towards the joy of living that God intended for us all.

GOOD MORNING SEAGULLS

The dawn that glows with peeping light
  Over distant hills and fields,
Blossoming away the night,
  That rosy gleam for ever thrills.

Wild birds stirring in their roost,
  Twitter greetings to the dawn,
Welcome daylight's warming host,
  Begin a chorus to the morn.

Gulls are flying from the west,
  Towards their daytime feeding ground,
Away from night-time's rugged coast,
  In measured flight without a sound.

Dipping, rising as they go,
  Thousands whirl on silver wings,
A white cloud tinged with sunrise glow
  Enhance the colours autumn brings.

With one accord they skim to earth,
  Then resting in the fields below,
Exchange the sea for soft green turf,
  Imitating drifts of snow.

The morning star fades with the sun,
  That rises now above the hill
With warmth and light for everyone,
  It's daily purpose to fulfil.

The cloud of gulls now rises gently,
  A swirling silver gleam of life,
Towards a ploughman's field of plenty,
  To yet return to sea each night.

LOYALTY

That mystical allegiance to someone or something that defies description by mere words, is in fact a form of spirituality, and spirituality itself defies description.

Loyalty manifests in all the higher forms of life to some degree, and it is impossible to draw a clear-cut line between a spiritual origin, and basic instinct for the purpose of self preservation of a species as would appear in lower forms of life.

"Birds of a feather flock together", so goes the old proverb. How can we know whether this comes into the realms of loyalty, or a basic instinct that holds a flock of birds together, flying, feeding or roosting? The fact remains that some birds follow this policy for living while some remain as individuals, and others as pairs. The cuckoo for instance, meets his partner, mates and goes on his way, whilst blackbirds meet, mate, and share the responsibilities of home and young until they can fend for themselves, thus displaying a sense of responsibility and loyalty.

With our limited knowledge we can only ask why there should be this difference in their moral behaviour. Undoubtedly it does fit somewhere into the realm of morals because we can see the same differential within the human race, although we do like to think we are on a higher plane of existence and thought. The fact remains that many animals of all kinds show these same differences, not only from species to species, but also individual animals within a species. Some foxes for instance are known to mate for life, displaying a loyalty not always seen in the human race, yet not all foxes follow this way of thinking either. Some birds, swans for instance, also display matrimonial loyalty, and of course many human beings also display this quality of thinking and behaviour.

A study of animal behaviour suggests that species which are basically loners living in pairs, are more likely to remain loyal to a mate than those that live in flocks, packs and herds. In that case the loyalty is more likely to be towards the group of which they are a part.

The human race appears to come somewhere between these two extremes according to the individuality and probably spirituality of each person. There does seem to be a wider range of loyalty within the human race than in other forms of life. On one hand we find those who prefer to live or work alone, sometimes in complete seclusion, whilst others show a tendency towards the herding instinct, for undoubtedly many people prefer to live, work and play in groups, and loyalty here can be less obvious and in some cases virtually non-existent. Where it does manifest, it may be towards a colleague in work, play, sport, marriage or friendship, or towards a group – a business, social activity or club for instance.

Loyalty towards others clearly has an important role to play in the quality of life on earth, and even survival. It can be witnessed between different species, occasionally in the wild, but more obviously within the domestic scene. A pet dog and cat for instance, living in the same home will often display loyalty to each other, sometimes in the form of protection. A horse will form a friendship with a different animal, perhaps a dog, donkey or goat, and will remain intensely loyal to its friend.

Dual species loyalty is even more common when one side of the partnership is human. Intense friendship and loyalty can build up between people and their pets, with dogs and horses in particular, and sometimes the greater strength of loyalty is with the animals. They have been known to remain loyal to an owner even though the owner lets them down in some way. Some animals, in loyalty to that human friend, suffer much pain or even death, such is their quality and strength of loyalty.

Through all the different manifestations of loyalty the world over, there emerges a slightly different aspect of this invaluable quality – loyalty to oneself. It is a far cry from selfishness and greed – that misinformed interpretation that some would choose to make. Loyalty to one's own self is an acknowledgement to conscience, the inbuilt knowledge of right and wrong – the still small voice within us all, too often deliberately buried to make life seem easier. It doesn't, failure to acknowledge conscience only postpones the day of enlightenment, meanwhile further crimes against our own personalities and consciences have been committed, greed or selfishness perhaps, thoughtlessness towards other life, or even cruelty. We produce for ourselves a weighty Karmic debt when we refuse to acknowledge conscience and loyalty – so intertwined that they can scarcely be divided.

The animal kingdom does not seem to have the same problem to any extent. Their faults and attributes are on a much less complicated level. They know when they are doing right or wrong and their minds make no attempt to disguise the truth, unlike human minds that too often seek to justify wrong thinking or seek reward or acknowledgement for right thinking. The simpler consciences of the animal kingdom do not create such problems for them.

As we ponder upon the many aspects of loyalty, perhaps we should reflect on the quality of loyalty displayed by so many of our animal friends and acquaintances. Perhaps, in their uncomplicated way, *they* could teach *us a* thing or two about loyalty – spirituality of the mind – that special something unseen that lifts some lives towards the wonder and bright light of the stars, the wonder we call God.

LOYALTY

– the anchorage
of
friendship.

UNIVERSAL LOVE

Love creates the depth of pure emotion,
   It teaches us the wonder of the stars,
Only true love knows the deep devotion,
   That brings the love of God to all our hearts.

The power of God is love in finest glory,
   With a million facets shining like the stars,
The finest diamond cannot tell the story,
   Of the many kinds of love God's power imparts.

It dances round the world with joy and happiness,
   The twinkle of a galaxy of stars,
To alleviate the pain of world distresses
   And illuminate the cruel and darker paths.

This universal love that God has given,
   To share amongst all life upon the earth,
Is the peace of mind that comes with loving giving,
   The vibration of God's love brings second birth.

Let all the many creatures of the world,
   Take the love that we are meant to share,
Let the flag of peace be lovingly unfurled,
   That the love of God may show us how to care.

OUR DOUBLE STANDARDS

There are few people who cannot raise a smile for a playful puppy or experience a tug inside themselves at the sight of a fluffy wide-eyed kitten. Even hard-headed businessmen recognise this and use these very facts to advertise their products, trying to persuade us to buy them, and succeeding to a remarkable extent.

Pictures of doe-eyed baby fawns, sentimentally labelled 'Bambis' after the one in the film of that name, and fluffy eared wide-eyed calves also promote oohs and aahs throughout the civilized world, and although their use as advertising material is for the same purpose, the end product will be very different. In the case of calves it will almost certainly arrive eventually on someone's dinner plate.

Meanwhile, those calves will have known the despair of being taken from the food and comfort their mothers supplied, experienced rough handling and crowded strange transport. Most will have only known life in cramped cages without the joy of sun and grass that God meant them to share with other animal life. Not for them the fun of running and skipping about in freedom.

When the Bambi grows up, it stands a good chance of being hunted to death, although it will in this case have enjoyed the growing up period with its own mother. It will not have suffered at the hands of mankind in the same way as the calf. In these modern times it may have grown up in farmed conditions, and this shy creature of the wild may have learnt to trust the farmer who reared it, unaware that it is destined to be slaughtered to satisfy man's craving for meat. Those doe-eyed stares of baby Bambi will become the wide-eyed stares of fear and betrayal, along with so many other animals that in babyhood tugged at our heartstrings.

Animals in their innocence and ignorance of mankind's double standards of thinking and actions, do not understand the hard lessons they have to learn in this respect, and in truth they should not have to do so, for if mankind is the superior being he imagines himself to be, surely he should by now have gone further along the road of compassion, according to the dictates of conscience.

It seems a very sad situation that many religions of the world do not teach greater compassion towards the animal kingdom, which inevitably puts some people with a greater understanding and consciousness towards that world of animals, in a difficult situation. They find their own religious teachers failing to give the guidance and help that they need, they can even find authority in conflict with their own more advanced knowledge in this particular matter. This can challenge both their own faith and the validity of their religion, resulting in doubt, confusion and inconsistency of purpose. If conscience is forced to be at variance with its own religious doctrines because they are of a different standard in some respect, then that religion may be failing in some way or other. Only the leaders of religions are in a position to improve that situation.

As we study the general picture of mankind's attitude towards animals, we find some strange anomalies and double standards. In the case of puppies and kittens, those fluffy bundles that give so much joy in their babyhood, many do grow up to be well loved and cared for as household pets, but many others would have a different story to tell if only they could speak our language. For a long time, the International Fund For Animal Welfare has been fighting to save dogs and cats from the same fate as our own calves and woolly lambs, for in some parts of the world they have been considered a delicacy for the human dinner table.

There has been much success in this particular aspect of human behaviour towards animals, but most of this success has been brought about by persuading governments to change their laws to protect animals, thereby protecting the reputation of the country involved. But for some people laws are made to be broken, and until billions of human minds learn to be aware of animal suffering and abuse, animals will continue to suffer atrocities at the hands of mankind. Education in spirituality appears to be the only answer, but we have to remember that the way of life and thinking in every country of the world is the result of its own particular culture through the ages, and culture is created initially by thought followed by habit.

Much progress has been made, much remains to be done, and we who live in western cultures, which we choose to call the civilized west, must be cautious of our criticism of other parts of the world, for our own double standards can blind us to the faults in our own culture and thinking. Our sentimental oohs and aahs at the sight of cuddly babyhood can turn so easily to calm indifference and cruel practices as age detracts from charm.

Modern factory farming methods, our slaughterhouses, some of our sports, our diet and many of our laboratories all leave a great deal to be desired, and in some respects are a disgrace to our claim to be civilized.

There are many aspects of cruelty that appear to be acceptable to some people who would themselves be indignant if accused of cruelty. Many very nice people still enjoy a traditional circus with its performing animals, and it is true that a few animals actually seem to enjoy displaying their tricks. Dogs for example will make up their own personal ones in our own homes or quickly learn and enjoy the games we teach them. When these are furthered for public performance by kindness and understanding, there may be no harm done. A dog will quickly display pleasure, fear or discomfort by the way it uses its own tail, so there is probably no harm in encouraging it to use its own talents as tricks if in fact the animal really does enjoy it.

When it comes to the larger undomesticated animals we have a very different picture. These animals are not only out of their natural environment, but are trained to do things which are quite unnatural to them. All wild animals seem to have an inbuilt fear of fire for instance, yet it is still possible to see a trained lion jumping through fire at the crack of a trainer's whip.

When one thinks of the sheer majesty of a lion or elephant in the wild, how can any right-thinking person enjoy watching them performing futile and undignified tricks in a circus ring? But some people still do, and would not agree that their thinking is wrong, neither do they take account of the cramped living cages these animals must endure in circus conditions.

Through the auspices of our television screens, most of us have seen a lioness fondling and caring for her cubs, while the male of the species looks on in a benevolent way, just like mum, dad and babies of any human family. We have watched giant elephants of some six tons, gently caressing their babies with their trunks and have delivered a few more oohs and aahs of our own at the Dumbos that trot contentedly at their sides in National Parks and wild places of the world. We then allow them to be hunted and killed for the sake of two pieces of ivory that happen to grow out of their cheeks for specific purposes of their own. Legislation and new laws are helping to stop this barbaric practice that would make the elephant extinct, but here again, only a more spiritual way of thinking will finally and permanently solve the problem, particularly amongst the people who buy or profit by the sale of the ivory, for someone will always want to flout the laws.

The tasks ahead are enormous, but much progress has been made. Not so many women these days enjoy wearing fur that should be where it rightly belongs – on the body of the original animal. When there is no demand and therefore no market for fashion furs, the killing will cease, and baby seals will once again look wide-eyed into the face of human beings without their trust being betrayed and their heads smashed in, and their skins ripped from their bodies whilst they still twitch and writhe in sudden death, some through careless killing not even dead. Lynx and the I.F.A.W. work unceasingly on their behalf.

Those lovely cuddly toys that we find in abundance in our toy shops should be an emblem and constant reminder that we have still much to learn, but each and every one of us can play a part. There are people out there willing and able to wade into the thick of cruelty and pain, willing to steel their sensibilities and emotions at the sickening sights they know they will encounter, the cruelties and the results of it that they will witness. The rest of us can at the very least support their courage and do our own part towards encouraging kinder, more spiritual thinking. We can give financial support wherever we can, and above all, set a good example in our daily way of life – by our deeds shall they know us.

The human race seems to have some kind of inbuilt herding instinct where the majority of people will want to be near others and copy them. One only has to watch the way so many people slavishly follow fashions, be it clothing, food, housing, gardens or interior decorating and furnishing, to realise the truth of this maxim. Therefore, we only need a fashion for kindness in every walk of life, for animals to be included in the happy and cruelty free results.

Let the Bambis, Dumbos, puppies and kittens of our world have a true meaning for us, so that our double standards will fade with our kinder knowledge, and cruelty eventually be an outmoded thing of the past as our spirituality looks towards a happier future for all life on earth. The human race will have taken great strides forward and left behind its double standards.

SANCTUARY OF PEACE

Spirit light will shine across the world,
The flag of peace will surely be unfurled,
When compassion reigns in every kindly heart,
And love creates its own redeeming part.

Let Spirit guide our ever hopeful dream,
And peace become our total living theme,
To help us play our own full part on earth,
Towards the perfect haven of rebirth.

May the animals that share the earth with man
Be free of fear according to God's plan,
And live together then in harmony,
That all may find their peaceful sanctuary.

ANECDOTES ON AN EQUINE THEME

OUR NOBLE HERITAGE – THE HORSE

Throughout Great Britain's History
  Of power, grace and shame,
There is one majesty of life
  That rises without blame,
Exemplary in the service given,
  Yet modest in its fame.

Proud battles have been fought and won
  Upon his broad strong back,
With heavy loads he's pulled and strained
  Along rough road and track,
Yet gently carried the child and weak,
  And overweighted pack.

With grace and patience he has served
  His master through the years,
No anger or cheap greediness
  Or unworthy hate or fears,
Just friendly courage freely given
  Through both happy times and tears.

Straight the furrow he has ploughed
  Through field and life alike,
He's towed the longboat through canals,
  Suffered the whip and brutal strike,
Dragged the timber, sown the seed,
  Proudly knowing the wrong from right.

The power behind each earthly throne
  Carried forth without remorse,
From tiny Shetland to Gentle Giant,
  Giving service without force
Is mankind's greatest heritage,
  The noble, majestic horse.

This poem aptly describes our friend and heritage on four legs – the horse. It makes us mindful of its superior qualities, and serves to remind us of our debt to this animal of power, gentleness and beauty. Perhaps it can also make us quietly aware of a few shortcomings in our own human natures, for the horse does not share them.

Their service to us through the ages is second to none yet many people think no further than it is service to which we are entitled from a horse. Its individuality is seldom even considered as would be with most dogs. To such minds it is merely an outmoded beast of burden, and an essential part of a cowboy film or equipment of a gypsy. It can be a useful status symbol, a membership card to a variety of sports and pastimes, and there for some people – it ends.

Fortunately, many others know the truth and see it with a different eye. It has been a loyal, integral part of our history and at this point of our evolution (and its own) the horse continues its service to mankind unabated, although often in very different ways.

No longer does it have to charge into battle carrying a heavy iron clad knight upon its back, it patiently carries disabled people – young and old, that they may experience the joy and independence of their association with a horse. This teaches much to the rider and helps to improve balance and muscle control, and gives a new dimension to lives that would otherwise be very limited indeed. These · activities are organised by the Riding For The Disabled Association.

In some parts of the world the horse is still carrying and pulling over-heavy loads. In too many places the stick or whip are still the only method of spurring the animal to greater effort. In western civilizations most people with a close association with horses know better, but still we see to our shame the use of whips and kicks to satisfy the human urge to win. Failure on our own part can sometimes promote anger that is taken out on the horse. Anyone who attends equine events or watches them on television has seen the occasional signs, and at such moments homo sapiens demonstrate the superiority of the horse.

I have never owned a horse myself, but have met quite a number through the years. My earliest memories revolve around a Suffolk Punch that belonged to my farming uncle. She was beautiful, proud and gentle and her normal tasks were concerned with ploughing, reaping and sowing, but when I appeared she stood patiently while I was lifted on to her back. I certainly enjoyed the experience and no doubt it was an easy way of passing the time for her – an interesting little diversion I expect. I also experienced on that farm the joy of travelling behind a horse as he trotted along to the milk factory with uncle's churns of milk. I can hear that satisfying clip clop of hooves down memory lane even now, and recall that bobbing head with ears erect and smoothly swaying shiny back, dressed in leather harness. These were about all I could see from the cart where I stood peering over the side, watching the grass verges and hedges passing by. Sometimes the hedge seemed so near I felt I could pick the wild roses and honeysuckle as we passed.

I was able to repeat this delightful experience many years later, on a horse drawn caravan holiday in Southern Ireland. I shall never forget Fred the skewbald who so willingly pulled our temporary home, nor piebald Katie our riding horse who was willing to take her turn on the flat parts when Fred developed a small harness sore which we were fortunately able to deal with ourselves.

Further back, I recall the milkman's horse, the stalwart of United Dairies, and I often wondered how he knew exactly where to stop and for how long. If the milkman took a little too long for the horse's liking, he would move on to the next customer and the milkman armed with rattling crate would have to catch up with him. Those were the days when the horse knew best, and therefore no customer was accidently forgotten. Coalmen had horses which would oblige in the same way; I remember once being near a coal depot and seeing an empty coal cart being taken along the road at a gentle trot – without a driver! It turned into the coalyard and stood outside the office. A man came out, helped the horse to manoeuvre the cart to stand in line with some others, unharnessed the horse and took him to the stables. Curious, I enquired about this mini pantomime and discovered that it happened every day. With the coal round complete, the driver would drop off at his favourite public house a short distance from the depot and the horse would complete the journey by himself, presumably by arrangement with the man in the office. You can't do *that* with an electric milk float or petrol engine coal lorry!

I once had a personal experience of the horse's ability to find its own way, when I was part of a carol and handbell party that toured our local villages collecting for charity. Apart from the village squares, we also visited outlying farms and large houses and made sure that rumours of the specific evenings of our ports of call preceded us. Country grapevines were very efficient at this sort of thing, and for that matter still are!

Dressed in the Victorian period, we travelled in a sixteen seater horse brake, our engine power being two strong horses. Many people living deep in the countryside not only contributed generously to our cause, but helped us through the frosty nights with ample supplies of mince pies, cider, ale and hot toddy. The further we went, the lustier the singing became. It was not until we arrived back at base one night, that we realised that our driver had been asleep for most of the return journey. The horses had in fact safely negotiated several miles of narrow country lanes, many with ditches on both sides, all by themselves at a nice gentle trot! As our base was not their real home, but only temporary accommodation, we were very impressed, especially as these two animals were unknown to each other in the normal way. We were grateful for their marvellous achievement in finding their way back over unknown ground, for it was not a regular route as in the accomplishments of the milk and coal round horses,we went to a different place each night, with only pale carriage lamps to guide. Most humans would be totally lost in such circumstances, but not our friends the horses, perhaps it was just as well that they didn't drink cider!

What I wonder, is so different in the thinking power of the horse that enables it to do these things, when we who consider ourselves their master – so miserably fail? Does it have a powerful sixth sense, or does it actually use its brain and intelligence, or maybe a mixture of both? Or – a further thought – was there in our case a guiding spirit that influenced our horses safely along that dark, narrow, but right route home. Who knows, perhaps our charitable motives protected us from possible disaster.

The horse as we know it today is very different to its wild ancestor, and the development has been more the result of man's interference than natural evolution. Unlike his manipulations with the dog, that influence does not seem to have weakened the horse, but merely channelled it into different directions, so that we now have horses of every size and for every purpose, from Shetland to Shire.

Perhaps this fact alone indicates the sheer strength and nobility of the horse, there can be few other animals that have not bowed down in either brain, mind or physique to the administrations of mankind, who is so careless in his attitude to animals.

Many a human life has been saved by a horse, the battlefields of man's foolish wars were strewn with the bodies of both man and beast, but while a horse had strength to walk it would carry its burden on to safety. It has climbed mountains for him, won fortunes at the races or taught him the foolishness of gambling.

There are now few truly wild horses except perhaps in some of the National Parks outside Britain. The wild ponies of our own Dartmoor, Exmoor and the New Forest are someone's property and are therefore at the mercy of their owners as much as the riding pony in a comfortable stable. If the owners of these semi wild animals choose to catch and herd them into a van en route to the slaughterers and probably a continental dinner table, the pony has no choice but to obey in fear at the betrayal of its trust. It is poor reward from the human race for the service that has been given through thousands of years. Horses have a wide field of vision and so we put blinkers on them to narrow their view for our own purposes. Perhaps we have blinkered ourselves in the process.

Fortunately there are many kindly souls who see the dangers and ignominy of extinction for various breeds of the horse, whilst others rescue the ill-treated and unwanted and so help to redress the balance as best they can. Such folk may take single action or support a charity that cares. I know of Reinbow's End Pony Reserve in Somerset, The Redwings Horse Sanctuary near Norwich, and two Shire Horse Centres in the West Country – one at St. Columb in Cornwall, the other at Yealmpton near Plymouth, whilst the tiny Shetlands are cared for at Moreton Hampstead in Devon. Without such places as these, it is likely that our equine heritage would be depleted and consciousness of caring could fade away.

Some people live their lives with much greater spirituality than others no matter what they call it – it is there for anyone to recognise, and if they wish – to emulate. It is by this example and leadership, often into uncertain pathways and sometimes despair, that some people help to raise the whole standard of thought and action towards a more humane way of life for everyone and everything. Such people already have the necessary courage, their need is for support, both moral and financial. Many are the calls upon our pockets, but many also are the tears that are shed for the predicament of suffering life on earth, and only we – the human race – can do anything to improve matters.

If half the people of the world were half as willing as the horse to serve with grace and dignity, this planet of ours would be a vastly better place in which to live, and its people worthy of the name Humanity .

A noble fact of life
Can help us run the course,
To guide us in compassion,
This fact is called – the horse.

A THOUGHT FOR THE FUTURE

May the conscience of mankind,
    Be expressed in caring love,
To ever seek for truth and find
    The peaceful message of the dove
To dwell in every heart and mind,
    Its honesty to prove.

May the peoples of the earth
    Learn peace within their hearts,
And find a spiritual rebirth
    As all evil thought departs,
That man may know the silent worth
    Universal love imparts.

May the sanctity of Spirit
    Filter into every troubled mind,
That love may prove its gentle merit,
    And anxious hearts may find
The love that has no limit,
    In the world that God designed.

LOVE ON FOUR LEGS

Many people do not consider that animals have the ability to love in the human sense of the word. This is basically because the human race has come to see sex as the main expression of love, when in fact it has little to do with it, sex being only one small way of expressing love, and in some cases takes place without love being involved at all. Sexual function is actually one of the very few basic instincts that mankind retains which is in every form of life from flowers to human beings, it is to ensure the continuation of the species, and in itself is therefore purely functional.

The misuse to which mankind puts it, is a basic cause of many of the world's problems – over-populating large areas for example, so that no reasonable quality of life can be sustained there without artificial help. When an area becomes over-populated with a species of the animal kingdom, they have their own ways of dealing with the situation. Weaker elements die off, the species or a part of it may move to a different place or adapt to different food or terrain. The human race will do something similar but often in the wrong way.

It is worth noting that when a population explosion occurs in the animal world, it is rarely if ever because of the promiscuous use of sex. It is more likely to be an attempt by nature to rectify a shortfall in previous years, and *those* situations often occur as a result of man's activities – over hunting for example, desecration of the environment and upsetting the natural food chain – hardly the administration of love in any language or circumstances.

Defining love – real love – is difficult if not impossible, it manifests in so many different ways. Caring, sacrificing one's self, loyalty, are all a means of expressing love. Generosity is another, especially a generosity of time, or even material things if one hasn't much to offer in the first place. Parental love, friendship, brother and sisterly love, love within marriage – the sharing and consideration – all these things are a manifestation of real love, and we can find animal equivalents in most of the more evolved species, which does of course include mankind.

Many a horse or dog for instance has saved its owner from injury or
death because of its loyalty and sometimes sacrifice. We know that
animals experience fear, yet an animal can overcome that basic instinct
in order to protect an owner in danger – a demonstration of love if ever
there was one.

Females with young will go to extremes to protect their babies. In
the human race we call it love, in the animal world we choose to call it
instinct. It is really a mixture of both in each case. It is a basic instinct
to protect the young of its own kind for that same old logical reason –
continuation of the species. It is also an expression of love because that
maternal instinct will protect its own personal family more than the
young of another family or species. When such an expression of love
does extend further than its own family, it becomes a wider form – a
compassion that begins to take on the attributes of spirituality, there
being no selfish motive involved. It is often found and recognised in
people but can also be seen in animals.

Compassion, the selfless caring for others, without questions or
conditions, service without thought of reward, perhaps it is here that
we find the nearest description of true love. It can be found anywhere
in the world amongst all the higher forms of life, and there is also no
part of the world where it is not sadly lacking. Where the lack of it
overrides the manifestation of compassion, wars, pain and suffering of
almost every kind are prevalent. Greed, inflated ego and hate are the
instruments of the darker forces that try to crush and eliminate the light
and love of compassion. Those who know and understand these things
are the standard-bearers of God who has given mankind the options,
the free will to choose, but needs the co-operation of people to
implement His cause. We can all further that cause by a more
compassionate attitude ourselves towards other people and the world of
all living things. We can take a lesson or two from the animal kingdom
itself, where service is often unconditional, ego unknown and hate is
rare. Even greed is usually because of some severe shortage, and in the
domestic animal is often replaced by generosity, pet dogs and cats can
be seen sharing food, beds or their owners' best armchairs.

Anyone who has had a much loved pet dog will have experienced
the loving enthusiasm with which they are greeted when returning
home, having left the dog to patiently await this highlight of the day.
There are many husbands and wives who would welcome the same

calibre of pleasure from their marital partners! Alas, humans create behaviour patterns of their own which do not always measure up to that of their pets. Even many cats, notorious for their controlled enthusiasms will often greet us with loud purrs and much walking round against our legs, a feline method of saying 'I'm glad you're back', which is another way of saying 'I love you'.

My friend Wendy had a cat who was prepared to sacrifice some comfort in order to greet her when she returned home from work. At a time when central heating was not in full swing for most houses, the hearthrug in front of the living room fire provided a nice cosy snoozing place for the family cat. But Wendy's mother vouched for the fact that Smokey would leave the fireside shortly before my friend was due to arrive, and sit patiently in the cold hall in order to greet her with the usual loud purrs and head rubbing against ankles technique. As cats are noted for looking after their own comforts first, it must indeed have been a true expression of feline love for a human being. Every word or act of caring says the same – "I love you". There are varying degrees of course as in everything else, but the message is the same whether it comes on two legs or four.

Horses too can demonstrate loyalty beyond the call of duty. Many an old soldier could tell of a horse that saved his life in wartime conditions. At present we do not know whether animals can estimate danger and assess risks, but we do know they experience fear and possess some kind of psychic power that enables them to be aware of danger before it arrives. In some instances it may be more attributable to acute hearing than psychic sensitivity, as in the case of anticipating earthquakes for example. On the other hand animals will become restless several days before an earthquake occurs, which would seem to preclude the hearing theory. What we do know, is that many domestic animals, particularly dogs and horses, will remain with their owners in such circumstances of pending disaster, rather than run away from it, which would be the natural action of their basic instincts. One has to accept therefore, that some animals under threat will display an affection for their owners through a special kind of animal loyalty, simply another kind of love. Not all humans can reach this height with their emotions and courage. Many a human has been abandoned in time of danger by other humans, where not only courage was lacking, but the love that would have overcome the fear.

Animals in the wild will sometimes go to extreme lengths involving the quelling of natural fear, simply to protect their young or partner, a very obvious example of animal love. It becomes increasingly clear that we have much to learn from the animal kingdom, for where their loyalty can rise above adverse circumstances, ours often lets both us and them down. I wonder what they think about it all when this happens?

There are some animals that on finding their special partner, mate for life, and this must surely be an area where mankind is falling short. The evidence of ever rising divorce rates and the ever increasing habit of couples living together for a short while and then changing partners, provides increasing testimony of a lack of personal responsibility, a self-centredness that is rarely seen in the animal world amongst those that normally create lifelong relationships. There *are* animals in the wild where the male of the species leaves the upbringing of young entirely to the other partner, but it is rare, and for the most part the more evolved animals stay in a family unit and share responsibility.

As far as I am aware, no scientific evidence has been discovered to explain why some animals display lifetime loyalty, and until irrefutable evidence is found to the contrary, I am content to believe that some kind of love is at the root of it.

Marriage itself is a man-made practice and therefore no-one would pretend that it occurs in the animal world. Through the years however, it has served us well in strengthening family relationships and securing the family ties that are needed for any kind of compassionate living. Animals that follow this way of life do not on the other hand appear to need any artificial ties of this kind, their own in-built sense of personal responsibility serves them well, sometimes better than in the human race.

We know that swans will mate for life. Having only two legs they do not really fit into this chapter but a personal memory of my own concerning them and this kind of devotion certainly does.

During my years with the P.D.S.A., I came across the following incident which would indeed put many a human relationship to shame. One of our ambulances was called to a lake where a swan appeared to be dying, and local people who habitually fed the wildfowl there were most concerned. The bird was easily captured, indicating the extent of its deterioration, and it was found to have injuries from a fishing line and hook which were also preventing it from feeding. An operation was successfully carried out and the bird was housed in a large shed to recover, but it would not accept food and quickly weakened still further. A second phone call then reported another swan becoming weak and refusing the food being offered. The ambulance service collected it from the same lake, but the vet could find nothing wrong with it apart from sheer weakness, so it was placed with the first swan with the hope that companionship of its own kind would help. It not only helped, it produced a complete cure for both birds.

Realizing that these birds were male and female, a few enquiries were made from the lady who had reported their plight in the first place, and she confirmed what we already suspected, they were a mated pair. While these two were together on the lake, the uninjured one stayed with its partner strong and supportive, but as soon as they were separated they both pined and lost the will to live. Once they were reunited, that will returned and gave them both the strength and motivation they needed. They soon recovered and were returned to the lake, and although this is no fairy story, I hope they lived happily ever after. Certainly they will live on in this book, providing for us proof that the animal kingdom does know the meaning and experience of love, expressed in this case by such loyalty that both would rather have died than live apart. They give another message too, calling for all anglers to be careful about leaving fishing lines and hooks on the banks of rivers and lakes, they are a real danger to wildlife and bring much suffering in their wake, sometimes in a way that most people would not consider possible – broken hearts.

When my friend Annabelle took a badly neglected and ill-treated cob into her foal and pony sanctuary in Somerset, she discovered she had rescued a 'boss horse' who became a self-appointed guardian of the fields, and 'foreman' of the other horses. Moonflower followed this policy through a hundred or so ponies and horses – in a nice sort of way that endeared him to Annabelle – who had taught the cob to trust again after the dreadful effects of the cruelty from the previous owners.

When April, another fourteen hand pony arrived, she was 100 per cent blind from the cruelty and neglect she had experienced, and Annabelle made elaborate arrangements to protect her, particularly from bossy Moonflower. She need not have worried, Moonflower turned her leadership instincts to good purpose by guiding the blind April and helping her with all the problems that blindness can bring. With loving care and veterinary attention some sight was restored, and Moonflower and April lived happily together, the one caring for the other in a way that is normally only associated with Guide Dogs and human beings, thus demonstrating that horses can also have the knowledge of compassion. In the face of such evidence, can we be so arrogant as to say it can't be so? Love is recognisable anywhere.

I can relate another case of similar circumstances between two dogs that belonged to my uncle. Pam was a young, large and gentle Alsatian German Shepherd. Patsy was old, a small Wire Haired Terrier who was losing her sight. She could get around reasonably well in daylight, but in the dark she was clearly very lost indeed. But Pam was ready to help and appointed herself unofficial guide dog for her smaller companion, demonstrating the ability of some dogs to recognise the need and to take to this kind of work naturally as part of a service they actually seem to enjoy giving.

The garden directly outside their door was tiny, but there was a much larger part on a higher level reached by several awkward steep steps. When these two dogs went out for toilet purposes at night, Patsy could feel her way *up* the steps in the dark but could not come down again. Pam would stand on the top step until Patsy came to touch her back left leg and Pam would then slowly negotiate the steps with Patsy being guided down through that contact and was able to follow Pam everywhere in the dark in this fashion. No human training was necessary, it was simply an expression of love in the form of compassion freely given by one dog to another. If only more people were as kind to one another as this, what a happy world we could be living in. A lesson in compassion for us all by love on four legs.

A BARK IN THE WILDERNESS

Throughout the history of mankind, his treatment and attitude towards animals has created a veritable wilderness of suffering and despair, not only for the animals themselves, but for the compassionate few of the human race who have been aware of that pain, and suffered themselves because of their attempts to help the world of animals.

At long last in 1991, we are beginning to see some great strides forward in the matter of greater kindness all round and this naturally includes more consideration for animals.

Consciousness of animal suffering is greater, action against the pain is increasing, while awareness of the needs of animals grows almost daily. But still it is left to the comparatively few dedicated strong people who either work on their own, maybe in small groups, or often as part of large charitable organisations dedicated to improving the lot of animals of all kinds. Without such people of awareness, the history of mankind in the matter of cruelty would be even more abysmal, it would by now have become a stench of evil that would be hard to eradicate.

As it is, the torch of compassion has always been held aloft by sufficient, kindly, more advanced souls, for the light to show a better way of living and thinking, so that the fruits of their labours can begin to ripen. The time may not be too far away when we shall see a harvest festival of kindness, the inevitable result of loving, hard work, and spiritual thinking. Some may have other titles for these endeavours, but the results will be the same. Good does triumph over evil in the end, because there are sufficient people of right thinking to make it so.

It is difficult to understand how mankind could have sunk so low in his attitude to animals, because he has always been dependent on them in some way or other, and it would seem to be a mere matter of common sense to protect anything so important to human existence. A brief look at the history of man's relationship with animals, suggests that fear and greed amongst the human race are probable basic causes, creating vicious circles of degradation that became ever harder to break, until enlightenment began to dawn on both a practical and spiritual level.

Religions that should have been the guardians of spirituality have often failed humanity in the matter of compassion towards both animals and the human race, encouraging wars, suspicions, fears, and sometimes cruelty in the name of religious festivals and ritual.

Much of this has disappeared in these more enlightened times. Sacrificial killing is mostly a sad blemish of the past, but there are still pockets of this unenlightened obscenity in the world today, often carried out in an atmosphere of jolly festivity rather than the sombre rites of long ago.

Even now the churches of the world rarely lead the teaching of compassion towards animals. The pioneers of kinder thinking are usually individuals who see the need and have the courage and strength to act. Churches, on seeing compassion in action through both individual people and organisations, usually support such efforts verbally, but still some of them do not accept the spirituality of animals or their survival after earthly death.

It seems that mankind still has a long way to go before he can feel himself to be among the saints, but the numbers of individuals treading the path of life in this direction increases daily. The plight of our animals in the wild, at some of our farms and laboratories, in our slaughterhouses and seas, and even in some of our homes, to name but a few, is gradually and noticeably improving. Although much remains to be done, the cry of the animal is at last being heard by more sensitive ears. The bark in the wilderness of cruelty and abuse is being heard around the world and across the oceans. The whimpers of the vulnerable and weak are fading slowly with the increased awareness of their suffering.

Triggered by our awareness of the need to conserve our environment, we realize at last that animals are a vital part of our own survival. The billions that have suffered and died for us and through us in the past, must not have died in vain. The bark in the wilderness is no longer just an appeal, it is a clarion call for courage and compassion in every corner of the earth.

THE FOX

Persecuted, hated, loved,
    Wherever do you fit
Into this human life of ours?
    For you are pushed around a bit!

Sometimes you are a naughty fox,
    Take *our* chickens for *your* dinner,
But you also eat the grubs and things,
    So we're really on a winner!

Secret wooded glades your home,
    Among majestic leafy trees,
Where bluebells ring and fairies sing
    Nature's song, with birds and bees.

But hark – the hunting horn I hear,
    Cutting through the air,
And you must flee your cosy den
    And run, I know not where.

And you must pit your wits my friend,
    Against the baying hounds,
Your paws fly faster than the hooves
    That pound across the ground.

Outnumbered you will be my friend,
    A hundred to one maybe,
But your wits are quick, the terrain is yours,
    So use them to keep you free.

With ears erect and brush held proud,
    Your beauty is undefiled,
So speed my friend your secret way,
    For God is on your side.

A PET'S EYE VIEW OF THE VET

I should have known when she called me. Instead of that sing-songy voice – "Walkies, come and have your collar on", it was just a dreary "Come and have your collar on" – the tone of voice tells a different story altogether. Then of course there's the car. It usually means we are going somewhere interesting, but occasionally it means the vet – just walking *never* means the vet, it's too far away and I'm jolly glad it is, I'd hate those vetty smells to be next door.

We arrived and I sat firmly on the back seat of the car, refusing to budge, all ten pounds of me. I know *that* because they sometimes make me sit on those silly scales and as they put one end on, I try to get the other end off. Its a bit of a game really to take my mind off what they might do next, but they never seem to see the funny side. Its just that I'm not keen on some of the things he does.

I eventually give in about getting out of the car, but I've made my point. We go and sit in that horrid waiting room, not an armchair in sight – well, *she* sits, I fiddle about, can't settle, and keep a wary eye on the other pets waiting their turn. That cat in the basket glares balefully out at me – thank goodness it *is* in a basket, I'm sure he'd have my ears for garters if he could get at me. Now that nice white persian over there is different, she's purring and although she has a rather superior, snooty look on her face she's O.K., she'd never lower herself to having a scrap. Mind you, him in the basket would I think, like to know her better, but she'd never lower herself to him either – or would she? The fussiest ladies are not always very particular when it comes to that – you know what! She really ought to be in a basket too, you never know what might happen in a vet's waiting room. Him in the basket has also got his eye on a hamster with that little boy, I wouldn't give much for its chances if him in the basket were not in the basket – if you see what I mean.

Oh dear, that's our name being called, so in we go, well actually in we slide, because I sit down to be dragged along as a matter of principle – you just have to let these humans know who's really the boss sometimes. Well, not *actually* boss of course, but we pets have to make our opinions known, and humans are sometimes a bit thick, so we have to make it pretty obvious as best we can.

Now we're in the vet's secret den, all bright lights and peculiar things. This is when I begin to wish I hadn't made so much fuss about a squiggly tummy and a hot dry nose. I'm sure a couple of blades of that nice long flat grass would have done the trick, but I usually get stopped from eating it, humans are so silly sometimes, and it would be cheaper than a vet anyway.

Now he's shaking that silly little stick of his – he does it nearly every time I come here, and I know just what he's going to do with it, and *that* is quite stupid today because its my nose that's hot, not my tail. I'll play my usual trick and sit down. It was heave ho on to the table to save the vet the trouble of bending down, and now here I am, tail being held up in a most undignified position, while he shoves his little stick up – well, you know where, I feel too upset and superior to mention it.

And I wish he wouldn't look into my eyes like that, he's no oil painting as far as I'm concerned, and I prefer her on the other end of my lead or that nice little bitch that lives down our road. Neither am I keen on that other thing he pokes in my ears, its cold and its uncomfortable, and I can tell him what's in there anyway, a little bit of wax and a wee bit of twig that I accidentally collected when I chased that rabbit into the bushes.

Oh well, that seems to be all over thank goodness, I can jump off the table now and make a dash for the door. A packet of pills and we're away, we'll deal with the pill problem later. I don't need them really, because I feel better now anyway, and I know where I can get hold of a bit of that grass on the quiet when we get home.

If I'm very good and look up at her in the right way I might even get a walkies after all.

Cheerio Mr. Vet, (he's really a very nice man), I know you do your best and sometimes I really do need you, like when I broke my leg – I was very grateful for your attentions then, little stick and all – but now and again we pets also know a thing or two ourselves, but you already knew that didn't you? Its just that I wish people understood better the way we think and the way we feel. Of course *she's* different, she *knows* just what I'm up to and knows I know a thing or two. Its a shame that some dogs don't have such understanding owners, and come to that –

such nice vets. I suppose they can't help having such peculiar toys to play with, I'd willingly let ours have one of my bonios to shake instead of that silly little stick – oh er – perhaps not, he might be daft enough to try and do the same thing with it and then I might have to *tell* him a thing or too!

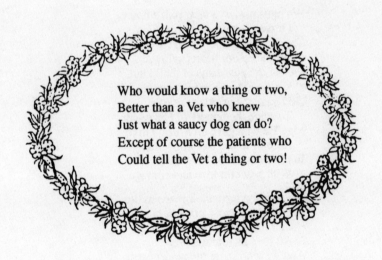

Who would know a thing or two,
Better than a Vet who knew
Just what a saucy dog can do?
Except of course the patients who
Could tell the Vet a thing or two!

COATS OF MANY COLOURS

Chatterboxes, every one,
　　In coats of many colours,
Spectacular their fancy dress,
　　But each looks like the other!
They brighten tropic forest glades,
　　And shriek without a pause,
But talk to lonely human beings,
　　So thank you dear macaws!
Every human in this world
　　Is a mix of good and fault,
Like bright macaws we should serve well,
　　Just like the Master taught.

We must preserve their forest home,
　　Or they'll have nowhere to go,
The wonder of their bright array
　　Will keep our hearts aglow.
We are the guardians of their kind,
　　We have dominion over them,
God gave the privilege of trust,
　　To share the bounty of His realm.
May He who gave all life and love,
　　Help us to use that knowledge
In preservation of His world,
　　With peaceful love and courage.

Macaws too have their place in life,
　　Their brightness lifts our hearts,
For all life has its part to play,
　　All love its role imparts,
And we who share the planet earth,
　　Can engender loving care
To every corner of the wild,
　　And preserve it everywhere.
May we be guided on our path
　　Through our allotted span,
Like bright macaws to play our part,
　　And do the best we can.

FOOD FOR THOUGHT

Modern technology is revealing an important aspect of food consumption – something that past generations have known almost instinctively, but for which they had little proof – people are very much what they eat.

The miraculous workings of the physical body utilizes in one way or another everything that we swallow. If we complain that we have indigestion, it is probably because we have given our stomachs the wrong food or drink, maybe over a long period of time or perhaps an isolated item. This can be a fault of our own in eating or drinking unwisely or accidently when we are unaware that food is in some way contaminated.

We can also fail to take in the nourishment we need, our bodies will react to the omission and ill health will occur, so here again, we are at least partially the result of what we eat, although in this case it is what we fail to eat.

The increasing recognition of allergy incidents to certain substances highlights the advantages modern man has over his earlier relations. He has vastly greater knowledge and use of advanced technology that promotes better diagnosis and treatment.

That same skill and knowledge has also *caused* many of the health problems that are experienced in the modern world. People living in parts of the globe where eating habits are simpler and more natural than those of western civilizations, do not seem to suffer the same serious health conditions, such as cancer, heart and circulatory illnesses.

Even in the veterinary world it is becoming increasingly obvious that pet and farm animals are affected by the food they consume. If contaminated food is fed to them they become ill, and sometimes the nature of that contamination is not very obvious. But we now know that an animal suffering from certain diseases can pass the condition on to other animals when they become food themselves. The common practice of using the waste parts of animal carcasses for animal foods is particularly suspect, and when we reflect that the best parts of the same carcasses are often used for human consumption, it is small wonder that people are subjecting their bodies to material with which they cannot cope.

All this is in addition to the chemical additives that we deliberately feed to both cattle and vegetation for the sake of greater profit. As we plough on through life adding ever more chemicals and medication to food on the hoof or in the ground, in attempts to right the wrongs of yesterday, we pile mistake upon mistake, until neither the human nor animal body can deal with the situation. Increasing numbers of allergies appear as the body of man protests, and our immunity systems break down under the strain. Even simple coughs, colds and sneezes become more and more common, in spite of increased knowledge and technology to deal with them.

Mysterious illnesses appear, some of them serious, whilst others are here today and gone tomorrow, like confidence tricksters of the medical world. How much of this devastation is due to the food we eat is almost anybody's guess at the present time, but it becomes increasingly obvious that our food and drink consumption can seriously affect our health - for good or ill as the case may be.

With the increasing awareness and rediscovery of organic farming and horticulture, mankind is making a move in the right direction, but the changeover is not easy. It is quite costly, it takes time to get good results and there are many adverse conditions to be overcome. Many people revolt mentally to what they consider a backward step, many are afraid to try. But 'People Power' has great strength, and as more and more people demand healthier food and are willing and able to pay for it, so the laws of supply and demand will come into operation, and better food will become available. It is for the general public to support those farmers and growers who are willing to try the resuscitation of an old and well-tried method. Too many people feel – without any real thought on the subject – that new is beautiful, old is ugly and useless, forgetting that some things mature with age and become of greater value as a result.

There is a strong case now for saying that some older growing practices come into this elite category. Our modern knowledge must be built on experience of the past, must sort the wheat from the chaff and use the best of both worlds, old and new.

There is another aspect to the move towards healthier eating, one that is becoming increasingly acceptable and practised – the phasing out of meat consumption, which would also help alleviate some of the world's undernourishment problems.

It is worth remembering that there are millions of people in the world who are underfed and undernourished, many of them actually starving. It is a known fact that many more people can be adequately fed directly from root and vegetation crops than when that same food is processed by an animal's body to supply meat. It therefore follows that if we express our compassion and love of animals by not eating them, we also demonstrate compassion and love for our fellow man – those people who not only have much harder lives than ours, but also do not have sufficient food to enable them to survive their hardships.

The sheer impracticability of the world population becoming vegetarian overnight must be obvious to everybody. It is surprising how often this fact is used as an excuse for not moving gradually in that direction. So much contamination is now known to pass along the food chain to humans via the flesh of animals, that its avoidance is a very obvious way to begin a move towards healthier eating.

Modern research has shown that people living a vegetarian way of life, are less prone to heart diseases, cancers of various kinds and circulatory problems. They have also been shown to be less susceptible to more minor illnesses, such as colds and sundry viruses that come under the umbrella of this description, when no-one knows what it really is.

We can next consider the ramifications between meat eating and the ethical reasons for not doing so. Many people feel quite simply that they could not kill an animal themselves in order to eat it, and that it is therefore wrong to expect anyone else to do it for them. Certainly a great many people would never touch another piece of meat if they had visited a slaughterhouse and seen for themselves the fear and pain of the animals, and the obscene gushing of blood that ensues. Calling the venue an abattoir in no way alters its function and ghastly results.

Likewise, most people visiting a factory meat processing plant would experience a similar revulsion, just as they would by inspecting a factory farm with its inhumane way of producing the meat in the first place. This is an area where the clock could so easily be turned back to great advantage for both animals and people, although the act of killing will always be an obscenity to truly compassionate souls. Legislation in Britain is moving towards a more natural life for farm animals, but there is still a great deal to be done. The sum total of pain and fear engendered by the slaughter of animals for food all over the world, bedevils the hearts and minds of truly caring people. We should surely weep with shame for this infidelity by the human race.

Many people do not realise that fear, frustration, anger and despair, can affect animals in the same way that it effects human beings. Chemical changes are brought about in the body and if that occurs in an animal destined for human consumption, the changes can be passed on to those who eat that carcass. It is a well known fact that a hunted deer, through increased adrenalin action, will produce tough meat unpleasant even to those who would normally eat venison, as against the meat of an animal that is shot unsuspectedly from a hide in the forest that is its natural home, where fear did not become part of the animal's reaction and killing.

Some religious sects still kill their animals for food by a procedure of ritual slaughter that would be quite unacceptable even to most meat eaters, and some of that meat finds its way into ordinary butcher's shops. There were once good hygienic reasons for these practices, but this is one area where the clock should not be turned back. Modern methods of killing, disgraceful though they may be, are usually a slight improvement when they conform to the law, in Britain at any rate. Unfortunately, slaughterers do not always adhere to those laws, with disastrous results for the animals.

Religion has much to answer for with its apathy towards the treatment of animals. In the past, ritual slaughter was common, and if in some cases the motives of the people were good although misguided, it does not explain the lack of spirituality and compassion that must have been prevalent at the time, and the lack of guidance from religious leaders.

Today we have no such excuses for the cruelty and pain that we inflict on animals in the name of either food or religion. Our taste-buds have been weaned on the taste of flesh, and many people find it difficult to break the habit, and find endless 'reasons' for not doing so. But it *can* be done and thousands of people are gradually turning away from meat, whilst some religions have always taught vegetarianism as a way of life, thereby setting an example that others could well follow. It is part of the Hindu and Buddhist religions for example, and the Bahais (a branch of the Muslim tradition) believe it to be a demonstration of the highest spiritual attribute, whilst the Buddhists believe the human being's treatment of animals to be a root cause of their aggression towards their own kind – worthy food for thought.

As the demand for meat decreases and the farm animal population falls as a result, kinder organic methods of rearing and keeping will be employed, and the life of farm animals will be greatly enhanced (the worthy objects of the organization Compassion In World Farming). With less demand on the slaughterhouse, it should be possible to improve conditions there also. Eventually, in years to come, they can then become redundant, or only used for humanitarian purposes, in much the same way as our vets often have to end life to prevent suffering today.

With the help of the Vegetarian Society, we can allow kindness and compassion to filter into our store cupboards and kitchens, so that the sum total of fear and suffering will decrease. As we consume less of the very food that carries the chemical changes caused by that fear, so we ourselves will be less affected by it. We will be healthier in mind and body, and with clearer consciences we will be spiritually progressing. The issue is not nearly so complicated as we try to make out. We are exhorted to show compassion towards all life – what could be simpler? What other reason do we need for giving our food more thought?

If beauty has a meaning,
Please let it blossom now,
Let compassion stop the
     screaming,
And beauty teach us how,

PAIN ON FOUR LEGS

It has always been a mystery to me that so many people do not realise the amount of pain that animals can feel. For some reason it is thought that they do not feel it to the same extent as human beings. Some animal life probably doesn't when the nervous system is less developed, but where this compares favourably with that of the human body, it becomes obvious that the same extent of pain must be experienced.

There is not one amongst us who has not known physical pain at some time in their lives, even a small cut or burn whilst we potter in our kitchens can hurt a lot. When we consider the obscene tortures inflicted by man upon his own kind we cringe with horror at the thought, and only heaven and the victims know what it actually feels like to experience such pain. In spite of this, it does not seem to occur to many people that our animals know physical pain in the same way.

As if that were not enough, many humans minds cannot accept the fact that animals can experience mental distress (at being let down by someone they have trusted for example), even more would dispute the possibility of spiritual pain, believing that animals have no soul and do not therefore have a spirit consciousness or body. Anyone who has had the good fortune to receive evidence of an animal's survival after death will know different to that.

Even people who own pets and sincerely feel that they love and care for them properly, often subject the animals to unnecessary distress, only because they do not understand that their pet has a similar nervous system to their own, that they do in fact function in a very similar way. Add a normal emotional distress factor to basic physical distress and it is easy to see the overall suffering that is often inflicted by animal owners who simply have not given sufficient thought and understanding to the subject.

Because of this, some pets suffer distress quite unnecessarily, dogs in parked cars for example. Many owners think that a window left open about one inch is enough for the dog's comfort, and it certainly is not, especially if the sun is likely to be out. It could be cloudy when you leave your dog but may not stay that way. In summer it may be hot even without the sun, or if the dog is large, it may well generate quite a lot of heat all by itself, and if there is more than one of them the situation is even worse. Dogs have a natural temperature that is higher than ours, and have no sweat glands to rid themselves of excess heat. Thus the panting dog with its tongue literally hanging out is using the natural way for it to cool itself, but owners should take special care if this is excessive or in a closed car, when exercising is obviously not the cause of the panting. If the dog is subjected to overheating, the distress can be enormous, heat stroke can follow and easily lead to death. Remember that a muzzled dog cannot pant anyway.

So owners should be very careful about weather conditions when leaving a dog in the car – even winter sun can cause problems. If it is absolutely necessary, the car *must* be in the shade and about four inches should be left open on at least two windows to create a current of air. Lattice type guards can be bought to fit into the top of the car windows, I would not consider them burglar proof, but who is going to be making such an obvious break-in with a dog in the car, especially if it is a large animal?

If a mishap should occur, emergency action is essential. Remove the dog from the car immediately and place it in the shade, the vehicle itself may provide some if there is nothing else available. Take the dog's drinking water from the boot (always carry some there, its cooler than the car) and gently pour or mop the cold water on top of the dog's head. Apart from the immediate effect of the cooler water, the evaporation will speed the effect. If the dog is seriously affected, pour cold water over its body as well, the prime requirement being to cool the dog as quickly as possible in any way you can. As soon as the dog is becoming conscious, dab water onto its tongue (which will probably be poking out anyway) until it can lap for itself. Do NOT pour water into its mouth, if it is unconscious, the dog would easily choke if the water runs into the lungs. If the dog does not recover quickly, you should seek the help of a vet immediately – you could save your dog's life. The best remedy however, is – don't let it happen in the first place. Try sitting in your car yourself in the same conditions, just to see how it feels, it is a good preventive exercise to save your dog.

The number of people who leave their pets shut in the house for hours at a time is unbelievable. Having no company they are bored and have no incentive to play, even if they are left with a pile of toys that would appeal in the ordinary way. They cannot get out to be clean, and even if this can be solved by a toilet tray, pet owners should ask themselves how *they* would like it! Young and healthy dogs especially, can't cope with this sort of frustration, and express their distress in a variety of undesirable ways. They may chew cushions or carpets or tear wallpaper from the walls. They are liable to ravage anything they can find and reach, books, newspapers, the cardigan you left on the chair, table legs, nuts, plants or that important letter you left on the table. I once came across a case where a dog chewed up an umbrella in its frustration at being left alone for half a day. A large dog, it was able to break some of the spokes, with disastrous results to its mouth, face and chest. It was fortunate not to lose an eye.

Young dogs can be gradually trained to be left for a couple of hours. Perhaps about ten minutes to start with, the time being slowly increased. We don't leave babies or small children unattended for hours on end, why on earth do some people leave their pets? We assume our pets have less intelligence than we have, but expect them to behave in a superior fashion! – Rather contradictory thinking on our own part to say the least.

When we consider the number of domesticated animals that are still left tied up, shut in sheds or outhouses, often without clean or comfortable bedding (sometimes none at all), possibly without even a bowl of water, still less with any concern for water to be clean, we have to accept that some people have much to learn about animals and the sort of caring that they need, plus a great deal to learn about their own quality of thinking.

But all this is dealing only with the simple thoughts and acts of daily caring, it does not even begin to consider actual cruelty in the shape of violence, administered through ill temper or sadistic enjoyment. Neither does it touch upon the suffering inflicted by unnecessary experiments, often for frivolous or cosmetic reasons that pander to human vanity, nor to man's preoccupation with greedy profits.

Horses and donkeys are also victims of mankind's neglect, lack of understanding and deliberate cruelty. Feet are frequently neglected areas, and laminitis can easily occur when these animals are put on to lush green grass in the mistaken belief that it is a treat for the horse or pony, but it can have serious consequences for the animal. Incorrect feeding and failure to worm are frequent causes of colic, causing great distress for the animal, and in severe cases the animal may die or have to be put down as a matter of mercy. Owners usually know about these things but do not take sufficient care, fail to make regular inspections, resulting in all sorts of unnecessary suffering.

From these strong and willing animals we often expect too much; too large a load, too high a jump, too great a distance and too much speed. They are often subjected to too much heat or cold, wrong or insufficient food, too little shelter, water, exercise and understanding.

The donkey is probably one of the most misused animals the world over, not only as a beast of burden, but as the recipient of man's brutality. In some parts of the world, it was once common practice to blind a donkey to make it more subservient to mankind's needs – walking round and round in a never ending circle, harnessed to a beam that worked a pump for water. It has probably been on the wrong end of a stick or whip more often than any other animal, yet, although it can be a trifle obstinate, its gentle nature makes it an ideal animal for children, otherwise it would not have become the great seaside attraction for them for so many years. But even here there has been abuse, too many overweight adults riding the animals for holiday 'fun' and rather silly photographs. Yet this is the animal that is accepted as being the transport for Jesus of Nazareth – so the New Testament tells us. Annually it is included in models of the Christmas crib for the wide-eyed gaze of little children, and the sentimental smiles of adults. For those who think about such things, our treatment of the donkey throughout time begins to make the human being look anything but human in our accepted sense of the word – more like a two timing monster without compassion or common sense, for who in his right mind would so ill-treat an animal that gives such excellent service? Many people treat their inanimate cars with better consideration.

The mule is another equine victim of abuse. Man is not only foolish enough to involve himself in the pain and horror of war, but is willing to use these animals in his man-made war conditions to carry and drag grossly heavy loads through the quagmires of mud and difficult terrain where nothing else could go, and horrendous injury often its only 'reward'. With his own life depending on the work and strength of the mule, it is perhaps understandable that extreme methods were often used to 'persuade' the mule to ever greater efforts, but there is no denying that the suffering of both were the result of war – brought about by man, for no animal ever started a war, they simply suffer from it helplessly.

When it comes to the infliction of pain, mankind wins hands down. Greedily, carelessly or deliberately he forces it upon his own kind and animals alike. Sport through the ages has been a vehicle for his cruelty, for it was in the name of sport that the Christians were sent into the arena to fight the lions with bare hands, it was considered sport to gamble on the chances of man versus animal with a variety of animal opponents. In more recent years the animal is always on the losing end, from hunting, trapping, baiting and fighting, not to mention equine casualties of the race course, where legs can be broken in a fall and the horse often has to be shot right there on the spot. Eventing course planners indulge in the challenge of pitting their wits against both horse and rider, making the hazards increasingly difficult to negotiate with ever increasing risk of injury to them. The motivation has changed little through the years, only the methods.

Bear baiting is illegal now, but bull fighting continues in some places, organised dog and cock fighting and badger baiting continues, to our shame, in dark secret places of our own 'civilized' country. In other parts of the world, dogs are still beaten to death whilst hung up like a carcass, so that their flesh will be more tender for human consumption, and cats are boiled alive for the same purpose. These practices are now illegal in South Korea, thanks to the efforts of the International Fund for Animal Welfare, but there are always those who are willing to break the law for profit. Rabbits, geese and other small animals are subjected to disgraceful pain and death in the name of religious festivals in Spain, while goats are tossed alive from church towers and donkeys hounded to death in public places in the same country for the same reason – the festive enjoyment of the participants – except of course the animals, for whom early death would be relief.

It is surely time that people – the superior race – actually became the superior life on earth that they like to think themselves to be. Much improvement has been made, many kindly steps forward. The veterinary world increasingly understands the psychological problems of animals, so that much professional help is available towards the reduction of distress for both animals and their owners. Organisations like the Royal Society for Prevention of Cruelty to Animals work endlessly on behalf of animals to reduce the dreadful cruelty and its effects. The I.F.A.W., working in a different way, takes on every aspect of animal abuse throughout the world. Thanks to hundreds of smaller organisations dedicated to eliminating cruelty in their own particular spheres of interest – from whaling and badger baiting to laboratory misuse, the pain is decreasing. Thanks to the individual concern and support of caring people all over the world who see animals as living, pain feeling life that is part of their own inheritance, part of the progression or degradation of the human soul, the cruelty begins to subside. But there is still a long way to go, many miles of compassion to traverse, many innocents still to suffer needless pain.

Thank heaven for the billions of kindly people in the world who carry the flag of compassion on behalf of the animals who cannot defend themselves, and who currently represent so much pain on four legs.

Compassion

is a gift

of love.

THE WORLD CAN SING

Such sadness we create whilst here on earth,
  Our foolish ways deliver too much pain,
But yet our power and common sense can shine
  To bring the light of mercy once again.

Let man create a world of happiness,
  And honest laughter be the key and goal,
Let cruel sorrow bow its head in shame,
  While joyful singing enters every soul.

May courage speak with every kindly word,
  And chase the darker forces into light,
That life on earth may find its place at last,
  In truth and rainbow colours shining bright.

Let compassion live in every thought and dream,
  And greed depart from every human heart,
May all animals and peoples of the earth
  Sing with heaven's love and happiness at last.

THE LAUGH'S ON US

Anyone who has had anything to do with the animal kingdom will know the necessity of a sense of humour. Nature has her own way of turning the tables on us from time to time, thus ensuring that our heads don't get too big for our hats. A sense of humour is an essential piece of equipment in order to satisfactorily negotiate awkward places as we climb the mountain of life anyway, and animals can provide us with excellent training, a valuable cushion of existence.

Much embarrassment can be overcome with laughter, many a hard knock is softened with a smile. Even sympathy can be expressed and delivered or received with a wry smile against ourselves, and members of the animal kingdom are past masters at giving us the ammunition to fight our way through adversity.

Anyone who has chased a wasp out of the kitchen door after much flapping and dancing around, knows perfectly well that it (or it's friend) can come straight back through the window. If the wasp had a thumb it would put it to its nose, if it had one of those as well. In the end you have to laugh to stop yourself getting angry.

Most anglers have a sense of humour, for how else can they deliver the fishy stories against themselves? 'The One That Got Away' series of tales has so many hilarious versions that most people will have heard of or experienced them first hand, but there are other humorous angles to angling that can tickle the sense of humour as well as the trout.

There is the one that just quietly *went* away. Whilst on holiday in Scotland, expecting a special Scottish catch, a friend of mine had instead caught one of the ugliest fish imaginable, known as a Pogge or Armed Bullhead, a huge head, long snout and long thin body covered in hard plates rather than scales, with a few sharp spines for good measure. Obviously quite useless as anybody's catch, for who wants a monster for lunch? This frightening fishy object had somehow to be released, so my now reluctant fisher friend allowed the line to go slack while he considered the situation – he was probably just playing for time and wishing he'd gone fossil hunting instead!

Eventually with courage more or less firmly in both hands, he drew the line in slowly, inch by inch, dreading the task ahead, until the bait finally appeared, minus the ugly duckling! In the clearer than clear Scottish water, it swam slowly away, having released itself from the slack line. Rumour has it that a loud chuckle came drifting from the river, while a sigh of relief was heard from my fisherman friend!

The one that *didn't* get away has also turned the tables on many an unsuspecting angler. This same good friend of mine went fishing with his boss, a Government Official. Failing to make a catch from my friend's usual fishing venue (a beach on the East Yorkshire coast), he suggested another spot not far away, where he felt their chances were better. In no time at all, a fairly large codling took the bait my friend had cast. It was reeled quickly in, until the last jerk was required to flick the fish over some timber stanchions that had stood the test of time and tide for longer than anyone could remember. The Government Official was supposed to catch the fish, but in the excitement – missed – the codling wrapped itself round his face and neck with a resounding, wriggling slap. Was my friend's face red? Of course it was, but whether from embarrassment or laughter, no one knows, and *he's* not telling, and its not really the best way to treat your boss. But Coddy certainly turned the tables on the fishers at the time and has provided a humorous fishy tale ever since. We can only hope the incident didn't tip the slippery scales against him.

My uncle's lively and enthusiastic Wire Haired Terrier provided much laughter and fun for everyone with whom she came in contact. One of her specialities was reserved for visiting us, or on her return home. Patsy would rush headlong into the living room, up onto the armchair, take a flying leap onto the settee, across the top of its back and down the other side, back onto the floor. She would then pause to take her bow at the ensuing laughter, for she was a comedienne of impeccable timing with her act.

One day things did not go according to her plan, because my mother had moved the furniture around and the armchair was not in the right position for Patsy's flying circuit. Alas, the nearby dining table was carefully laid for a birthday party tea, as my mother and aunt shared the same birthdate, and I can pin-point this event to 23rd June, because they always shared the celebratory tea of strawberries and cream. Patsy was forced to land directly on the settee, dashed across the back as usual, but was presumably aware that something was missing from her routine.

In an attempt to rectify this, she took a flying leap onto the table, flopping right in the middle, where she stopped to look around and take stock. Not too much damage was done, apart from a few bruised strawberries and a leg hole in the trifle! But a great hush hung in the air for a brief moment, until we all burst out laughing, for we had indeed enjoyed this perennial joke of Patsy's for several years, it was our own fault that on this occasion it went wrong, so the laugh was truly on us.

When Patsy performed the same trick on her return home on an earlier occasion, things went wrong when again furniture had been moved (humans hardly ever learn from these experiences). This time she dashed into the only handy opening – up the chimney! It was one of those cast iron fireplaces with a round hole and closeable plate at the back, with considerable space each side of it. Fortunately the fire was not lit, or there certainly would not have been the laughter as Patsy's little white face – now jet black – reappeared cautiously in the opening. She stepped carefully out of the fireplace on to a nice new fireside rug, soot all over, until a good shake deposited it all over the room. We laughed so much, we hardly had strength to clear up the mess! If *only* that furniture had not been moved, but it was, and once again the laugh was on us.

Many an animal has suffered a reprimand when something has gone wrong that is not really the animal's fault. Creatures of habit, just like ourselves, we expect them to know when we ourselves have altered the circumstances. Sometimes they show remarkable intuitiveness and are aware of a difference, even as we can be, but it can't be relied upon in an animal any more than we can be sure of it in ourselves. It is strange how on the one hand we can regard animals as our inferiors, and then expect them to have greater foresight or even intelligence than ourselves. Somewhere along the line, we humans are not always as logical in our thoughts as the animals over whom we consider ourselves superior. This very fact is a situation when the laugh is often on us!

TWO HEADS IN THE CLOUDS

(Or a tongue in cheek tail!)

Two little dogs were sitting on a cloud, looking at the view of their old home on earth and watching their owners working in the garden.

"Have you noticed" said Bonzo, " – that they've cut down our favourite tree?" "Yes," said Fido, " – but they've left a nice bit of trunk, and I think it will sprout out if its watered well."

"Well they won't have time down there, and we haven't got a watering can, so we can't do it either," said Bonzo. "No," said Fido, "– but we can jump about on this cloud and make it rain, then we can get that dog that lives next door to go in and fertilize it!"

ANECDOTES ON A CANINE THEME

Throughout the ages of mankind's partnership with animals, he has presumptuously assumed that the animal kingdom lives by instinct and without the ability to reason and make assessment for action as a result of it. It is only in comparatively recent times that some enlightened minds have cast doubt upon this theory and are now beginning to assert more positive thinking on the matter, and actually in a few cases set out to prove the 'new' theory.

Pet owners have known about animal reasoning power for a very long time and have adequately proved it to their own satisfaction if nobody else's. Meanwhile the scientific mind is somewhat behind-hand in this respect, mainly because they seek the answer to the question of 'how' rather than 'whether' – metaphorically putting the cart before the horse, and there is little point in the 'how' question if the original concept is not already acceptable as a fact. In any case, whoever heard of a horse pushing a cart – they are designed to pull! – and adequately exhibit their own particular reasoning power in the process.

It is the ability to reason and apply the results of it to current circumstances, that is largely responsible for the characteristics of each animal in the higher orders of earthly life, and is very obvious when it reaches mankind. When this is added to the spiritual development of the individual, the characterisation becomes even more obvious in all the higher forms of life. A kinder disposition can manifest, or a more generous nature for example. At the other end of this scale, jealousy or intolerance may be displayed, all of which are indications of character in both humans and many animals, which begins with the ability to think and reason, and act according to the development of each unique individual, for no two are completely alike, even identical twins in either the human race or animal kingdom develop their own characteristics according to this power to reason, and their degree of spirituality.

Once one becomes aware of this attribute in animals, pleasure and wonder in their company is greatly enhanced. Most of the knowledge of animal behaviour has been acquired through the work of animal trainers and those who study it from a medical and psychiatric point of view. From their efforts much has been learned, but it is mostly with the object of controlling the animals in some way or other, perhaps their behaviour, their use to mankind or for commercial purposes. Many are the theories and explanations given for an animal's reaction to a variety of circumstances. Seldom is an animal given credit for thinking, reasoning and consequential action in its own individual right. Yet every observant pet owner knows that animals can and do think for themselves, they are as individual as every human being.

Through the years domestic animals have been programmed to act in certain ways in certain circumstances, thereby leading many people to believe that all animals of a species conform to the patterns imposed by man, thus losing some of the evidence and knowledge that lies hidden now below the surface.

Pet owners everywhere will recognise the natural traits and behaviour patterns in the following anecdotes with dogs as the centre piece. Elsewhere in this book, cats will add their quota of proof for animal powers of reasoning. But here we shall see how an animal can go beyond the thinking power for which we habitually give it credit. We shall learn in the process that every expert theory can be challenged in the light of the individuality of each animal, precisely as it can be challenged with individual people. Add to this the fact that all life also has some basic instincts, mostly associated with two situations, self preservation and the survival of species, and we begin to realise the complexity of the whole subject. But here we are only concerned with a few simple proofs of the power to think and reason in the canine world of pets.

Alsatian German Shepherd dogs are usually noted, not only for their intelligence, but also for loyalty and guarding. The following experiences with one of my own, not only proves all three attributes, but demonstrates the ability to reason and act on that reasoning with very sound judgment – I would venture to suggest, beyond that which might occur in some people! They also demonstrate how that thinking can prompt action not normally associated with this particular breed.

Judy was a delightful black and tan of medium build and a great sense of humour, another quality not often recognised amongst dogs. I related in our previous book, *Memory Rings The Bells* the following two incidents, and make no apology for repeating them for the benefit of readers I have not met before.

Our lodger in an upstairs apartment was the proud owner of a brand new baby and had taken him with her to the village shop a few hundred yards along the road, leaving the pram outside the shop. When she came out of the shop, preoccupied with thoughts of her shopping and not being used to the pram, she proceeded to walk back home without her new offspring. Normally she left the pram outside in the back garden whilst she went upstairs with her purchases, and Judy would guard the pram until she returned. But on this occasion – no pram! no baby!

Judy rushed upstairs, executing a sort of canine jig or polka in her attempts to get mother's attention, until at last in sheer exasperation, lodger with dog in tow arrived in my kitchen, with clear 'help' expressions on both faces. Surprised at the mother's return with no baby in view, I guessed the rest and enquired where he was. Her face was a momentary study of horror. "My God", she gasped, "I've left him outside the shop". She duly retrieved the baby with no harm done and Judy settled down to await the next bit of excitement, whilst enjoying the praise and reward for a job well done and well thought out.

Much later, the same baby, now toddling by himself, was exploring the garden, unknown to me, and momentarily unknown to his mother who was hanging her washing on the line some distance up the garden. Judy rushed into the kitchen to coax me outside to find young Roy peering into our fairly deep goldfish pond with a large island stone in the middle of it. He was fascinated by the fish that were looking for a free meal. Judy was warily watching the child from a respectable distance and I was watching both with a mixture of horror and amazement – he was bent almost in half in his curiosity with the fish.

I quietly called his name, so as not to startle him, whilst Judy remained still and silent, well away from the scene of potential calamity. Roy turned and smiled, pointing to the fish, while I coaxed him to come towards me. Only when he had actually started to walk away from the danger, did Judy run in and stand guard between the baby and the pond. This must surely demonstrate a high degree of thought, reasoning power and restraint. One false move on her part could have precipitated a dreadful accident, yet I spoke no word of command to her, she was not a trained dog for such circumstances but thought the whole thing out for herself from beginning to end.

My third anecdote concerns some thinking by Judy, this time for herself. She had nine puppies and they were growing nicely, still feeding from her and were a bit of a handful to say the least – perhaps I should say pawful! She decided to give herself some respite by leaving them in their bed alone, whilst she herself rested on the floor outside the bed. However, it was a cold concrete floor and when I spotted her there and realised her reasoning, I told her she couldn't lay there like that, I'd get her some sacks to lie on for the time being. I was on my way to the same old clothes line and intended to get the sacks on my return, but Judy forestalled me. When I got back to her, she was trotting out of a lean-to beside the house, dragging a sack she had pulled from a pile of folded ones heaped on top of an old oil drum. To my amazement she had already acquired one and positioned it beside the puppies' bed, and here she was collecting a second. She knew what I had suggested, knew where to find them and simply reasoned she might as well do it herself.

In contrast to the well-known guarding instincts of the breed, Judy exhibited a gentle reasoning power and skill that never failed to impress me, although she gave me one or two nasty moments before I learnt to trust her power to think and act accordingly.

We were on a smallholding in the days when broody hens sat on a clutch of eggs and hatched them into chicks. They were then deposited in a small and cosy hen coup with a wire netting run attached. The problem with these D.I.Y. chick nurseries was a fairly frequent occurrence, and came about because mother hen liked to scratch about for grubs and things, a perfectly natural part of a chicken's life. In her enthusiasm she would often scratch out a hole in the ground against the bottom wooden rail of the run, thus allowing the small chicks to escape, and believe me they are not so easy to round up once they have discovered the delights of playing hooky and defying Mum's anxious clucks!

But Judy was master of this situation. She would herd them into a corner, much as a sheepdog herds sheep, catch one at a time in her mouth and bring them to me with their heads sticking out from one side of her mouth and their feet protruding from the other. She would drop them dry and unharmed into my hands.

She was also an expert egg collector. Free-range chickens often tend to lay their eggs in secret places rather than the nestboxes provided by considerate and hopeful poultry farmers, thereby of course exhibiting a crafty little bit of reasoning power of their own. It is then up to the farmer to pit his wits against those of the chicken and defeat her little games – often he succeeds – well he *should*, shouldn't he? But I had a great advantage – I had Judy! Untrained and unasked, she would find these nests in secret places and bring the eggs to me one by one, with never a crack or squash although she did in fact enjoy eating (or rather slurping) a raw egg!

Her habit of searching under the raspberry canes for a juicy ripe one I had missed, was another of her demonstrations of the power to think. She would inspect the one she had found, and if it was not quite ripe, she would leave it and examine it again the next day until it was almost ready to drop. Only then would she pluck it and eat it. I know it doesn't really sound like food for Alsatians, but then of course, *that* is just the problem, we train our pets as a breed and as individuals, and expect them to conform without deviation and forget that they too have the power to think, to reason, and act accordingly.

Perhaps we could sometimes take a lesson from these members of the canine race. There are many times when we human beings fail in these very same things – to think and reason before we act – if we did, many a disaster could be avoided, and figuratively speaking, many a baby wouldn't fall into the pond after all.

That animals possess a sixth sense that is stronger than our own is such a well-known fact that few people would dispute it. Cats in particular are credited with being psychic, but dogs can also exhibit this mysterious trait that has so far defied reliable explanation and the investigations of researchers. The following canine anecdote is a perfect example.

It was 15th August, 1952, and a good friend of mine was holidaying at Lynton in North Devon with her husband, and accompanied by a friend and his Bulldog. The friend had planned to go on a little further and stay at a hotel down by the sea at Lynmouth.

But a problem arose, Champion Vanessa had other ideas, exerting the full weight of body and mind, she flatly refused to go. With the typical obstinacy of the breed she had decided to stay put, and equally typical of so many dog owners, he agreed to stay at Lynton.

That was the night when flood waters roared down into Lynmouth demolishing cottages, killing more than 30 people and causing enormous damage. The hotel where Vanessa and her owner would have stayed had they continued their journey was among those most badly damaged.

There must have been gratitude all round to Vanessa for her purposeful refusal to change venues, but her motive will forever remain uncertain. Did she simply want to stay with my friend Edna and her husband Fred because she liked being with them, or was her doggy psychic power sensing the oncoming disaster?

It depends on one's knowledge and beliefs whether one opts for the former explanation or the latter, but it is odds on that Vanessa knew of the coming danger, because she had no reason to have any particular allegiance to my friends, so that a loyalty or particular affection towards them could be virtually ruled out. It would seem to be just another case of an animal knowing a thing or two that we humans can't always match.

The devotion of a dog is its special gift to all humanity.

IT'S ALL IN THE AURA

(Or a sniff in time saves a lot of trouble)

Two little dogs were patiently waiting while their owners chatted outside the baker's shop.

"Do you think we'll go to heaven when we die, like humans do?," asked the Yorkie of the Poodle.

"Of course," said the Poodle, "how else will they know when there are undesirable characters about trying to get in?"

"That's all very well," said Yorkie, "but how will *we* know who's good and who's bad, it will be rather a big responsibility sorting them out."

"Easy," said the Poodle, "same as we do now, take a quick sniff at their auras."

"Gosh, yes," said Yorkie, "the baddies won't stand a ghost of a chance with us there!"

PAUSE FOR THOUGHT

For many people speed has become of the essence – a god of their own making that propels them into action when a pause for thought would reveal a better way, perhaps a kinder way – certainly a wiser one. Speed in its rightful place can achieve much that is worthy of the effort involved. In the wrong place, like everything else, it can bring disappointment and even disaster.

At this time in the history of mankind, when brilliant brain power has produced and developed technology to a point where it seems to be taking over the human race, and is increasing its rate of progress beyond that which mankind can control, it is perhaps a time to pause for thought. Maybe we should allow ourselves time for our minds to develop in the hope that they can catch up with the work of the brain and thus create a balance of ideals.

All life as originally created was part of a balanced existence, but homo sapiens, with its enthusiasms and privileges, has failed to keep that balance. Greed, selfishness and outrageous ego has created an imbalance that becomes increasingly hard to control. Mistakes born of technology, instead of being reversed are attacked with further mistakes, and thereby enlarging the problems rather than curing them.

The results of this mismanagement can be seen in almost every aspect of life on earth, simply because mankind has allowed brain power to move forward faster than the consciousness of mind.

Through the ages various outstanding people have called upon the world at large to pause for thought, appealing to mankind's better nature, but although that world has heard the voice and the message, it never seems to react. That same world still refuses to think deeply enough to take the massive action that is required.

There is a gradual increase in the number of people whose consciousness and spirituality has been stirred by the devastation and cruelties that have become acceptable facts to other less enlightened souls.

Sometimes a disaster, either natural or man-made, will cause us to pause for thought in the mêlée of today's daily living. It is dealt with as best it' may with the brilliant technology we have discovered and developed, but the conscience is barely given time to consider the deeper implications, the inner message of disaster. Mankind in his foolishness does not respond at the same quickening rate as his own technological creations, so that balance is never restored.

One hears the argument that we cannot go backwards, cannot escape from these advancements of the past, which is perfectly true, they are there and mankind must live with that fact. What is overlooked or blatantly rejected is that mankind's spirituality should have developed at the same or even greater speed as the technical march forward, then a balance could have existed that would enable mankind's discoveries and developments to be put to wonderfully good use, instead of producing the disasters that have plagued the world for so long.

The brain of man has produced many wonders, the mind of man does not know how to use them properly, not from lack of teachers, but a wilful determination to disregard their message.

The message these advanced minds bring is always basically the same, and is simplicity itself – love one another. A few do, too many don't, and others respond sometimes, usually when it suits them to do so. Meanwhile the enemies of love – that iniquitous greed, selfishness and inflated ego, smother the world in a fog of self-destruction and suffering. Yet the light of loving compassion refuses to die, gradually it increases, manifesting in the increasing number of people who band together in a variety of common causes, all aimed at rescuing some section of world life from pain, degradation or destruction. In such folk we see the light of love gradually burning ever brighter, with a warmth of illumination that can yet save mankind from himself. But such is the speed of creative technology, that the rate of growth in spirituality must increase enormously to even keep pace. To catch up on lost opportunities even more effort is required. So the possible avenues of advancement must be recognised and used so that a proper balance of brain and mind can be created, then evil will be gradually dying away, seen less often and to a decreasing degree, and the beautiful world that was originally intended will rise like phoenix from the ashes, a triumph for mankind, and those people who have given so much – sometimes their lives – towards the loving purposes of God.

The senseless slaughter of body and crushing of mind must cease, even though it must inevitably be a gradual process. That process can be speeded up to stop the rot of degradation that is the present malaise of mankind. It is not too late to pause for thought, and in the peacefulness of that pause, the voices in the wilderness will be heard more clearly, for they have never died, only become smothered by the cacophony of discordant noise that seeks to smother the voice of compassion and universal love for life upon the earth – people and animals alike.

The world of animals makes no war upon mankind, nor does it seek to abuse it, only the human race has the power and knowledge to find and use the necessary spirituality to bring about the changes that a pause for thought can bring. The Animal Kingdom can only follow and be an integral part of such a heaven on earth.

Every flower speaks of life,
All life speaks of God,
God teaches us the power of love,
And love could save the world.

A PLACE IN THE COLD

The wild white places of the Arctic Regions have beckoned man ever since he first suspected they were there. Men of courage and curiosity wended their way towards the poles in the spirit of exploration, and with the help of the Husky Sled Dog to tow supplies for the journey, he opened up a host of hidden wealth and wonder that put Pandora's box to shame, and equally let loose upon the world yet another opportunity for good or ill.

Mankind was not equipped by nature to live in these vast areas of snow and ice, and had he stayed to merely look, listen, love and depart with honour and curiosity satisfied, much pain, sorrow and human degradation would have been avoided.

But once the human race had cast its greedy eye upon these great white wonders of the world, the stage was set for yet another horror story, directed, acted and applauded by people, whose brains and souls were meant for much worthier causes.

Whales were chased and harpooned in a sea of blood and courage on the part of both hunter and hunted. Later with the increased technology for which mankind is renowned, the whales could be killed with much less risk to their human slaughterers, so that the meat and oil of this majestic mammal of the seas could be plundered at an ever greater rate, until some became in danger of extinction.

Thanks to the efforts of the Whale and Dolphin Conservation Society, Greenpeace, and the I.F.A.W., there has been a halt to the killing of whales except for scientific purposes, but at this time of writing there are moves from some countries to regain international agreement for the slaughter to start again, and meanwhile the horror has continued under the cover of scientific research, where even little children can join in the red excitement of the kill, and few people really believe it is entirely in the name of science.

The majestic giant of the snows, the polar bear, is also on the brink of extinction through mankind's 'superior' knowledge. As soon as technology produced powerful enough guns and suitable transport, the polar bear was shot, sometimes for meat, but mainly that his beautiful pelt could adorn the wall or floor of some baronial hall, the silent head to lay stuffed and grotesque, teeth bared and soft white ears crumpled unnaturally with rough human usage. Man's misplaced pride watches the animal pace its artificial home in zoos, an understandable situation in the early days of the polar bear's discovery, but with our current skills in photography, an unnecessary indignity for such a dignified animal.

Penguins seem to have been spared much attention by man, presumably we have not yet found much financial gain for ourselves in these birds. We have become fond of them because of their upright stance and the fact that they make us laugh. Anything that can bring innocent fun to our world has to be a welcome part of it. Let us hope that we do not discover a way of making bounty out of penguins. The Southern Hemisphere would be a sadder place without them and mankind will have dipped even lower in spirituality if he is the cause of the downfall of these unique birds of the cold.

Seals on the other hand have suffered at the hands and minds of man to an appalling degree. In this case we have not even the merit of believing they provide a necessary product for mankind's use. The slaughter of seals is almost entirely to satisfy a craving for luxury furs at the demand of high fashion in the 'civilized' world.

Some people find the feel and look of fur irresistible, and when this is channelled towards caring for animals and loving them for their own sake, this can produce a special kind of loving compassion. When the motive is wrong, the result is a desire to actually wear that lovely soft fur themselves, so that slaughter has to take place to rob the animal of its skin, and vanity overtakes compassion, careless of the suffering that brought the furs to the shops in the first place.

Thanks to the efforts of a number of charitable organisations such as Lynx and the I.F.A.W., and the courage and humanity of many kindly people, these practices are gradually dying out. The tide of opinion is turning away from fashion furs at last, particularly in Western countries. But those who profit by the sale of seal skins are finding other markets where compassion has barely broken from its own eggshell.

If anyone really thinks that these killings are done in a humane way, they should certainly explore the subject further. I do not wish to upset my readers with the gory details here, sufficient to point out that baby seals do not understand the cruelties of man, and do not therefore make any attempt to escape. On the wild ice floes there are in any case no hiding places – nowhere for them to even try to go. These babies, born of their mothers in the same way that human babies find the light of day, simply sit there while their killers perpetrate their bloody tasks, and the parent seals, having no way to defend their young often sit and cry or try to cuddle up to the skinned remains of their babies.

Take just a moment of your time to imagine this happening to human beings in some place where it was considered that over-population and profit were sufficient licence for such behaviour.

Now the human race is turning greedy eyes upon the hidden minerals of arctic regions. Fearful that someone else will get there first and reap the gigantic profits of such mining, nations cast wary eyes around these cold and wild places, like thieves guarding a loot that is not yet theirs. If mankind cannot co-operate with himself to preserve these last frontiers of the wild, we shall open up a box of self-destruction from which there will be no turning back. These desolate places in the cold must belong and be shared internationally, preserved as a shrine to compassionate common sense. Meanwhile the whales, polar bears and seals suffer and die, waiting for the human race to find its own spirituality.

The silent white majesty of the Arctic and Antarctic *must* be preserved. The cry on the wind in storm ridden gales, the crack of the ice when the sun adds its strength, the call of the seal in the ecstasy of breeding time – these are the lonely calls for help that we *must* hear, or turn deaf ears to our cost.

Mankind already knows the solutions, and only he can put them into practice. The arctic regions may well be our last opportunity to come to our senses and use God's gifts to us in the way He meant us to use them, to preserve our environment and all life in it, so that our sojourn on earth may be a university of spiritual achievement. It is for us, here and now to use these places in the cold to cool our greedy ardour, justify our presence here and demonstrate to our Maker that true humanity is yet a name of which we can be proud.

A PLACE IN THE WILD

In the wild places of the world,
  Nature's lonely secrets hide and dwell,
From mountain top to arid plain below,
  And churning sea to quiet forest dell.

No man should ever spoil the quiet haven,
  Where lizard pokes his ever nervous head,
Or deer be startled from their silent browsing,
  Nor hedgehog turfed from leafy winter bed.

The buzzard flies the wild and windy moorland,
  The dolphin plays and leaps around the seas,
While polar bear will guard his icy homestead,
  The koala nibbles eucalyptus leaves.

All the wild places of the world,
  Are needed by the fauna that is free,
Man takes this land for over-population,
  The folly of his greed he cannot see.

Let curlews cry the plea for isolation,
  Let nature keep some places undefiled,
May the finer side of man respond with greatness,
  And guard the secret places of the wild.

THE HEALING POWER OF ANIMALS

It is a very obvious fact that our relationship with animals can have a very telling effect on our own lives. A fact that we often accept without question or any inclination to consider how or why. The therapeutic effect that animals can have on us humans has been realised in an offhand sort of way for so many years that it is probably impossible to see where it began. Possibly it didn't actually begin at all, but merely evolved along with the rest of man's progress. It is quite possible that in the early days of mankind's evolution, when hunting animals for food was the main preoccupation of the head of the family, he may have brought home the occasional very young animal because he had killed its mother. One can imagine his own young children welcoming the orphaned baby, and the little girls in particular exercising their early mothering instincts. Maybe these were the first pets, and we can feel fairly confident that these young helpless animals had a good therapeutic effect. We must draw a veil over the next part of their lives, it was probably short as man exercised his own power over them.

It is only in recent years that doctors and other people involved with the caring of elderly people, have come to realise the value of having an animal as part of the equipment. They now accept that being able to stroke an animal has a soothing effect on many people, helping with heart and nerve conditions, depression and instabilities of all kinds. There are people who, unable to communicate with their fellow human beings, can in fact blossom out to an animal. It has been known for someone with some inner psychological block who cannot or will not speak, to suddenly begin talking to an animal. Many a child that has been through a very serious illness, exhibiting apathy and a reluctance to get well, will respond to an animal. Somehow the animal can communicate its own enthusiasm for life and spark off new hope and enthusiasm in the child.

Little if any research has been carried out to find out how or why this happens, the fact remains that it does, a fact for which we should be heartily thankful if nothing else, for many people have benefited by this strange phenomenon.

A few easy theories have been expressed, some experts think the effect of stroking an animal is purely in the mind of the person. There are in fact people so afraid of some animals that they couldn't bring themselves to stroke one anyway, but this is surely too simple for such a complex matter, for this principle could be applied to ordinary medicines, what suits one patient doesn't necessarily suit another.

There is also the very valid point that not all animals have an apparent ability to project a healing quality. Dogs and cats seem to be the most likely animals to have this gift, and it may be connected with their well known psychic power. It is part of the make-up of clairvoyants and human Spiritual healers and it is therefore logical that the same power in animals would have a similar result.

It is difficult enough to prove spirit or psychic healing power in people, indeed – from a scientific point of view it has not been proved, only results provide sound evidence. In the case of animals it becomes even more difficult. Yet many people will testify to the fact that they have felt better after being with an animal. If this *is* purely an emotional or psychological reason for the betterment, we have to ask how the presence of the animal prompted it. As yet nobody has offered a satisfactory or conclusive answer to that question.

There is however a certain amount of circumstantial evidence, some of which has come my own way. Some years ago, I used to sit for absent or distant healing in my bedroom, and always sat in the same chair. I was not able to do this at any set time of the day, but I could guarantee that my Yorkie dog Tina would appear and jump on my lap. There she would stay, sitting upright with her back towards me until I had finished my session of healing. She would then jump down and go about her own business without more ado.

I have known her come in from the bottom of the garden to do this, and I always had a curious feeling of greater power when she was there. Strangely she did not continue the habit on a regular basis after I had moved to another home, when my healing seemed to be replaced with spirit writing. Theories come to mind for this but no specific explanation. I feel certain in my own mind that Tina had some kind of healing power, coupled with a telepathic instinct to know when I needed her to use it – or was she guided to me almost daily, at the right time, by yet another unseen hand of Spirit, and if so, what knowledge did she have to pick up that guidance and act upon it?

"God moves in a mysterious way His wonders to perform", someone said once upon a time. Wonders they certainly are, mysterious they remain, and animals are a part of that wonder and mystery.

Research into the area of animals has brought so much suffering to them in the past, and indeed still does, that it is to be hoped investigation into the realms of healing by them will not attract attention further than idle curiosity and gratitude. It is one area where faith alone must be sufficient, for what would be gained by experiment in this particular field? It is already proving difficult to stop all experimentation for cosmetic purposes on an international scale, in spite of stalwart efforts by a variety of organisations such as Beauty Without Cruelty, the British Union for the Abolition of Vivisection, and Frame. Such experiments are clearly a gross misuse of our power over animals. It is to be hoped that it will not be too long before men of science will use their skills to find ways of experimenting and gaining knowledge without the use of live animals, so that medical knowledge will be furthered for people and animals alike, without the dark shadows of unnecessary pain. The Humane Research Trust already sponsors such work very effectively, and there is no reason why such a policy cannot continue and increase. It merely requires money and the open-mindedness and dedication of scientists who care, who are willing to travel this different route to the alleviation of suffering in its widest sense. When experiments on animals for cosmetic and material profit are banned world-wide, we will be well on the road to a complete phase-out of the practice of vivisection altogether, as new, better and kinder methods will be discovered to replace the old. As the doors for frivolous and unnecessary experiments close for those who work in this area of science, necessity for alternative methods will prod medical research and the larger business firms into finding those better systems.

The healing power of animals must not include suffering for ever. When people want to do something enough, they find a way to do it, and here, conscience must be their guide. If animals can indeed project a healing power for our benefit, then we must use our own powers of persuasion and healing compassion to protect them and the gift they offer, otherwise we are taking from them and offering nothing in return. Perhaps, some day, their healing power will infiltrate sufficient human minds to heal the conscience of the world. A dream perhaps – perhaps not.

THE ANIMAL WORLD AND SUPERSTITION

Some animals have through the ages, acquired an unsought and undeserved reputation for bringing harm to people in the form of bad luck, ill health or even death. Most of this has been brought about by human beings themselves in a variety of different ways and for an endless string of different reasons.

A great many people are afraid of bats for instance, quite unwarranted, and a partial cause of bringing some of them to near extinction. The actual causes are loss of habitat and the correct food, brought about by mankind's own ignorance (use of pesticides etc.) but a strong contributory factor is the fact that most people do not really care about bats enough to do anything on their behalf, and that is because of the fear they unwittingly engender.

Bats do not for instance become entangled in people's hair, their strong inbuilt radar system would guide them away from the owner of the head of hair, bats have no inclination at all for such unlikely traps. The fact is that the speed and sometimes erratic appearance of their flight suggests that they do not know quite where they are going and what they are doing. In fact their mastery over flight and purpose is almost phenomenal. The erratic flight is because they are homing in on darting insects on the wing, thus causing the hunter to follow this apparently unstable flight, the sudden and unpredictable changes of direction cause fear in the minds of mere people. The fact that this all happens at night or in the mysterious evening shadows when human sight is inefficient, only adds to the fear – humans like to *see* what is going on around them. Add to all this the reputation of witches in days gone by, and their supposed use of "leg of frog or toad and wing of bat" for some of their nastier spells, and we have a perfect platform for a fear and therefore hatred of bats.

Fortunately for bats, much more is now known about these little animals of night-time flight. We now know that some insects that can be a nuisance to mankind are food for bats, and much safer than any pesticide. We also know that their reputation for evil, killing, biting and bloodsucking human beings is unfounded. Only three species of the one thousand or so in existence have feeding habits near to this belief. The vampire bat makes a small incision on the animal of its choice and takes a small amount of blood for its own food. When this procedure has been monitored and carefully observed, it is obvious that the host animal is usually quite unaware of the bat using it as a sort of jungle Take Away. The animal does not miss the minute quantity of blood the bat has had for supper, and all concerned are quite happy – except of course the unenlightened human, who in ignorance and fear, refuses to believe such simple explanatory facts.

Horror stories, especially when presented on film, add to the unwarranted fears, and man's own desire for excitement adds to the unfortunate reputation of the bat. Some of the species look ugly to our human way of thinking, and this can also cause revulsion, but their design is perfect for their needs, their apparent ugliness is in the eye and mind of the human beholder, certainly not in the mind of other bats of their species.

Fortunately for humans and bats alike, more recent investigation has revealed their true worth to the balance of nature, and the traditional fears and misrepresentations of the bat are being dispelled as many more people become aware of their value and needs. The Bat Conservation Trust has given great strength to the real facts and image of these little winged and harmless creatures, and much is being done to preserve their habitat and food. If some of the larger bats, known to the imaginative mind of human beings as flying foxes, also manage to survive, then there is reason to be grateful for the wonder and resilience of nature, that it has somehow managed to survive in spite of the ignorance of the 'superior race'. The V.W.T. Bat Project, based at Paignton Zoo, co-ordinates the work of numerous local bat preservation and rescue organisations for the very purpose of enlightening the public and dispelling the fear of bats.

Ill omens, bad luck, and all manner of dreaded human disasters are attached to members of the animal world, even when common sense tells us that such ideas are foolish. In these cases, it is probably mind over matter that causes our human problems, rather than the number of magpies or crows we have seen. If we believe strongly enough that something unpleasant is going to happen, we create and attract to ourselves the kind of vibrations that are liable to bring about adverse circumstances. We can do exactly the same thing with good luck omens. If the appearance of a black cat across our path lifts us into the right frame of mind to expect some good luck it will probably happen, because our own minds have been sufficiently lifted for the right vibrations to be attracted and effective.

If some of these things, both good and bad, really do seem to happen according to folklore beliefs, then most people who do not believe these things offer the word coincidence as an explanation, we are then forced to ask ourselves – what is a coincidence? A set of circumstances that appear to have connections with one another, without any known logical explanation. This leads us to the possibility that there *is* a plan, negotiated by an unseen mind and unknown hand. There seems to be no reason why animals cannot be a part of those plans, or because of the psychic sensitivity of many animals, why they should not be aware in advance of potential good or bad 'luck'. Extrasensory perception does just that in the human being, so there can be no reason why it should not have the same effect on animals.

It is traditionally believed that a howling dog foretells a nearby death. This does not mean that every time a dog howls such a death will occur, there may well be other reasons for its howling, but if a death is about to take place, a nearby dog may well pick up the vibrations or receive some kind of precognition and howl as a consequence. I had personal experience of this when my Alsatian Lucy suddenly lifted her head and howled loud and long, in the middle of the lawn. Two days later our neighbour died rather unexpectedly.

The dog never howled again, and I never knew her to do so before that occasion. This is therefore an instance where the dog probably did know in advance of a pending passing.

In past times, witches often had a cat as a 'familiar'. These animals are known to be psychic, and have many mysterious tales told about them. Many people are afraid of cats without knowing why, as there is rarely a known cause of the fear as in the case of dogs, so perhaps some people have an instinctive knowledge of the cat's psychic ability, and people tend to fear what they do not understand.

Many birds and other animals are associated with the matter of luck, both good and bad, and strangely, the effects often vary from one country to another. In Britain for instance, to see a black horse is considered lucky, but it is unlucky to see one in France. The French theory would seem more appropriate because of the use of black horses for funerals in the past, and occasionally they are used even in these modern times.

Sometimes an old superstition is carried forward into present-day use for a different purpose from the original. Plaiting ribbons into a horse's tail for instance, is done for decorative purposes now, but in days gone by its purpose was to foil the spells of witches. The logic behind such superstition usually remains a mystery, but in the case of the horse, it is known that the animal was an object of worship in ancient Greece, and some of our more recent superstitions about the animal may stem from those past times.

It does seem that in a few cases there is a logical source for mankind's superstitions and strange beliefs. Most appear to be based more on the power of the human mind to *make* something happen because of the strongly held belief that it will be so – mind over matter. It is easy to see how one section of the community, in times past, was able to influence others in this way – an early type of brain washing. Witches for instance, being able to promote fear and manipulate the thinking of others. In modern times, this manipulation is more likely to come from advertisers in newspapers, magazines, or more directly through television. If we are told something often enough and strongly enough, we tend to believe it. The witches of old seem to have been well aware of this, and used animals and birds as their media. The use of psychic power in both animals and humans only adds to the mystery of superstitions and the part they play in the evolution of mankind. It is however clear that we all have the power of thought to overcome the groundless superstitions that affect us today, leaving us only with the prophetic occurrences that have some sound logic as their base. Our difficulty is in sorting one from the other, and for this we must rely upon our own instincts and psychic knowledge. We fortunately have wiser minds in the world of spirit to guide our reasoning – if we will only listen – but even here, these more knowledgeable minds are able to teach us through our association with animals, for they are the ones that seem to have retained more of the instinct that can protect, guide and foresee, they truly do seem to know a few things beyond our own knowledge, a knowledge that maybe we once had, but in our carelessness, have lost.

ODE TO A TOAD

How see you now to find the snuggle of brown leaves,
With eye half open from your lonely winter sleep,
How will you find the slug and beetle that you need
For living, and all the springtime life and love?
The other eye must surely open wide,
Peruse the dampened grass and cold brown mud,
And seek the hidden treasures of your own domain,
That you may offer to the lovely lady of your choice,
The richness of all nature's home and springtime loving
Can spawn to life more than a thousand baby toads.
Peer now again at the warming sunlight glow,
And scuttle off to find your ever-waiting mate.
Swim the pools and creep beneath the sheltering winter grass,
And sing your song of annual invitation,
For she will hear and follow through your call,
To supplement the value of your breed, at nature's instigation.
See now dear toad the beauty of your quiet world,
For you are part and parcel of a life that we can share,
We will protect and honour your domain,
To prove to you and heaven that we really care.

FUN ON FOUR LEGS

Many people do not realise that animals have a sense of humour. Like us, their sense of fun varies from animal to animal, and different species express their sense of humour in different ways. The human species has the greatest variety of expression, but animals certainly have their own inimitable ways of expressing their sense of fun.

Compared to dogs, cats often have a more macabre sense of humour, just as some humans do. Many cats like to play with a live mouse they have caught. They will pat it around, maybe toss it in the air before killing it. Other cats will follow the same procedure of play but then let the mouse go free. Kittens often follow this pattern – perhaps they have not had time to learn to kill, which is lucky for the mouse because a kitten's play is usually quite gentle, especially with the females. We can see this pattern of behaviour in small children. Boys in particular will play attacking and stalking games. It is not until maturity sets in that viciousness – even to killing – can manifest itself in just a few. Kittens are usually content to play more innocently with pretty, gently moving inanimate objects, leaves or feathers blowing in the breeze, and human babies like soft toys that dangle within range of touching, but sadly these delightful traits disappear all too soon and a more violent humour replaces it.

Dogs on the other hand will play with inanimate objects well into adult life, in fact a ball or rubber ring can be a pleasing toy for as long as the dog is capable of running and jumping about. Unfortunately dogs do not recognise the hidden dangers of some 'toys'. Stones for example can easily break teeth or be swallowed, as any veterinary surgeon can tell you who has had to operate to remove a seaside pebble. Sticks are another danger. They are such a handy 'toy' when out for a walk with the dog, and of course dogs love to retrieve them and toss them around, but if caught in mid-air or carried with the end of the stick pointing out of the front of the dog's mouth, it does not take much horrified imagination to realise what can happen to the other end of the stick – puncturing the palate or back of the throat are the most common accidents. Fun on four legs can turn to disaster on four legs when pebbles and sticks become improvised toys and are best left where they belong – on the ground.

Most dogs do however have a good sense of humour, which of course varies with each individual animal, just as it does with us. Apart from playing with their own toys, most dogs like to share their games with owners or anyone that is prepared to join in, and it is here that a light-hearted battle of wits can indicate a real sense of humour, for dogs love to tease us, even if we do think the boot is on the other foot.

Many dogs will retrieve a thrown toy, bring it back for another throw, but then run off with it again – with many a backward glance that clearly says, "Come on, come and get it". This invitation to chase the dog is in sharp contrast to the natural habit of chasing something itself, and indicates the desire for fun by teasing us, because we are never able to actually catch the joker until the dog chooses to let us do so. This teasing on the part of the dog not only indicates its sense of humour, but demonstrates a sense of timing that is not often attributed to dogs, and could well be emulated by many humans, whose sense of timing with jokes on other people can fall far short of common sense and kindness.

Adult cats usually play their games on their own or possibly with one companion of its own kind, although some cats can be coaxed into play with humans. Kittens on the other hand play their rough-and-tumble games together in common with the young of all multi-birth animals, including those in the wild. In this case it is a training ground for their needs in later life, catching food, self defence, protection of territory, home and family. It is a basic instinct left in domestic animals of multi-birth, although it also appears in the infant play of the young of single births, as in lambs, calves and in the human race, so once again we see similarities between people and animals that are not apparent at first glance.

So we see that whilst cats rarely develop their play beyond individual amusement, dogs often use their reasoning power to conjure up games of their own, frequently seeking to involve human friends and owners in the games. We ourselves have a classic example of this with our very small Yorkshire Terriers. Daisy, the larger of the two has ping pong balls as her favourite toys. She never carries them about for chasing games, preferring to press them tiddlywink fashion with her paw to jump them around the room. The next step is to pick up the ball and find a hiding place, beneath an armchair for example, although a favourite spot is to stuff it into our electronic organ pedals, pushing it well down in attempts to hide it. She then comes to persuade us to find it – the old well-known childrens' game 'hunt the slipper'. Meanwhile, Poppette is standing in the wings so to speak, awaiting our move. When we do, she rushes in to help, whilst Daisy takes time off to rush to her dinner bowl, and gobble up some of the contents. It is Poppette that gathers the ball, tosses it away ready for the next round of fun, and then attends to her own dinner bowl. This game can go on for as long as we or they are willing to play.

Animal behaviour experts would probably dismiss this game simply as attempts to get attention. Certainly our attention and involvement is a necessary part of the game, but I insist that it goes much further than that, for both dogs know easier ways of gaining attention! It becomes a team game between two people and two dogs, each dependent on participation by the others. There are several phases to the game, some dog-made rules and a well thought out plan that is adhered to each time it is played. The choice of hiding places also indicates some careful thought, and Daisy has discovered many, including my serviette ring which I sometimes toss across the floor for her amusement, she will then very carefully drop the ball into the ring. Such hiding places for the game do suggest a well thought out scheme to have fun, with a recognizable plan at the root of it. People do it, who are we to think that dogs cannot? They can and they do.

I once had an Alsatian Shepherd dog whose favourite little game was to 'steal' something from someone's pocket, and then display the object to show what she had done – with high glee! She clearly didn't want the object she had taken for herself or any other purpose than to have fun. Lucy was a veritable pickpocket, and no-one was ever aware of her antics until she presented them with the object she had taken. It was a simple fun game that required some planning and quiet sleight-of-nose action on her part.

I remember a horse years ago that developed an amusing trick whilst being led by its owner. By walking half a pace behind the man, the horse was able to get his nose behind the man's head and under the brim of his hat. He then lifted the hat and tipped it over the man's eyes! It was a regular fun and games trick that the horse had thought out for himself, and I swear he had a big horsey grin on his face when he had done it!

Apart from the training play of young animals in the wild, adults also have their own variety of fun and games. Bears look unlikely candidates as comedians, but Grizzly's seem to enjoy sliding down snowy slopes much as a child would, whilst Black and Brown bears prefer to roll and somersault their way downhill. Otters also like slides, will make their own mud ones and proceed to use them repeatedly with obvious delight. Badgers on the other hand appear to prefer more organised games and have been seen indulging in their own version of boxing, purely for the fun of it, whilst foxes tend to adopt more doglike amusements and will toss a piece of moss about, shake it, pounce on it, just as a dog would play with a toy from the pet shop. Almost any small object may be used in this way, apparently to amuse itself, because it is difficult to see what other reason the fox could have for this light-hearted little activity. Even deer have been spotted playing games of tag and hide and seek, maybe with different rules to the human version but recognisable just the same. It seems that a sense of fun is not the prerogative of people, but an inbuilt gift for some of them and some animals as well.

If we stop to think about it, any pet owner can recall amusing instances of animals displaying a sense of humour, it must be very frustrating for them when we fail to see the funny side. Most of us have had the experience of telling some little jokey tale that has amused us, only to find it doesn't click with anyone else! Animals share so many emotions with us, so why not this one? We really ought to make more effort to understand their disappointment if we fail to laugh at their jokes, and their pleasure when we appreciate them. After all, laughter and innocent fun are good for the soul and daily living whether it is on two legs or four.

A SMILE
can heal a wound of the soul,
or soothe an aching heart.

LESSONS IN PATIENCE

"Patience is a virtue, possess it if you can, its seldom found in woman and never found in man". So went the old proverb that grannies loved to quote to their impatient grandchildren. But it isn't really complete – its originator should have added – "often found in animals, so copy if you can", because the animal kingdom very often exhibits an enormous amount of patience.

Watch any domestic cat waiting to pounce on unsuspecting prey – a mouse from its hole in the wainscotting or a small bird perched in a garden shrub waiting for breadcrumbs to be thrown on to the lawn. The cat knows the routine and patiently just waits.

Observe a pet dog on its lead, waiting patiently whilst its owner chats to a friend they have just met on the way to the shops. Bored the pet probably is, impatient it is not.

Wild animals display the same self control. The lioness stalking her prey is never hurried, she doesn't make hasty false moves that will defeat her purpose, but waits patiently, gently edging her way to the best position for attack, thereby demonstrating not only her patience, but her ability to think out the best moves for the particular circumstances she has at that time, and her patience will enable her to carry out her plan with the greatest possible chance of success.

Pet dogs have infinite patience with their human owners. They may let you know when dinner is late, but won't throw a tantrum about it, and there's many a wife who can't attribute the same consideration to her husband – oh that he would see and follow the example of his own dog!

Animals seem to have this in-built knowledge that makes life so much more comfortable. They only exhibit impatience in conditions brought about by man, or sometimes in excitement when some longed-for event is unduly delayed, and who would dare blame them for that?

There are so many lessons that could be learned from the animal kingdom – patience is just one. Yet we still persist in considering them far beneath the human race on the evolutionary scale. In some respects perhaps they are when measured by the human yardstick, but on the spiritual level they have much to teach us. By their example we should know them, but too often we do not wish to see or understand. There must be times when we stretch their patience to its limits.

If we at times must have patience with the animals in our care, it is but another way of learning through them ourselves. The busy rushing of daily life for so many people can preclude the pause for patience and calm consideration. But the chaos we endure can be of our own making, the animal world is wiser in its patience.

Patience
is a
silent
strength
of
mind.

TOLERANCE

Every truly spiritual teacher through the ages has taught the need for tolerance and compassion. Too often they are woefully lacking in everyday life. Even those of comparatively high spiritual achievement can fall foul of this particular trap. The reason is not hard to find – like a coin of the realm, toleration is double sided.

There are times to be tolerant and other times when some *in*tolerance seems called for. Compassion is the guiding star, so that we clearly have to use the two in unison. If tolerance of a given situation permits pain and suffering for others, then it must have the wrong motivation.

If we see a child or elderly person being attacked and robbed, we would be failing the principles of common decency and compassion if we did not attempt to help. In helping we would of necessity have to be prepared to protect ourselves and possibly use some kind of physical force in the process – a clear case of intolerance for the right reason. The same situation can be stepped up to international levels. It surely wouldn't be right to stand back and watch a small community or country attacked and browbeaten by a larger one for its own gain, without going in to help the weaker, and violence on a very much larger scale would be almost inevitable.

When animals come into such a situation our assessing abilities are pushed even further. Often we can find ourselves in a situation where we are forced to choose between animals and our fellow human beings as we try to decide where our tolerance and loyalty should lie. Now we suddenly realise that tolerance and the right motivation are not always enough – loyalty has entered the picture, and loyalty is yet another high spiritual attribute that can present its own difficulties.

For those who believe that animals are of little or no consequence to our own being, there is no problem. For those who do not think they can feel pain and distress the situation does not even arise. For those who believe that mankind has carte blanche to do as he wishes with animals – that they are merely there for his own use without any consideration on his own part, conscience will have no meaning where animals are involved, still less any tolerance towards them.

But for those who are treading a spiritual pathway and therefore accept that animals have their own rightful place in the world, feel pain, can suffer distress and humiliation, the question of tolerance can become a complicated issue.

In the case of wild animals for instance, what right have we to destroy their habitat and food for our own use? Is it really tolerable to hunt them to exhaustion, death and even extinction for our own pleasure? For those who like to quote the Bible to back up a cause, it says that man shall have dominion over them, authority which suggests looking after them rather than destroying them. Before the wording in the Bible was changed, and misquoted in the book of Common Prayer, it also clearly stated in the Old Testament Commandments "Thou shalt not kill". It is therefore surprising that so many people who follow the teachings of the Bible, tolerate the killing of animals for human pleasure and purposes. It becomes necessary to be tolerant towards those who cannot see this strange anomaly. In fact, many minds only recognise the facts they wish to accept, ignoring the ones that are difficult or uncomfortable – old habits die hard. It is surely right to show tolerance towards this kind of thinking in our fellow man lest we ourselves fall into the same trap in some other field of endeavour. Yet the question then arises – how much tolerance can we spare for the suffering of animals that are the victims of that thinking? It is the personal responsibility of each one of us.

In the end, we can only do our best according to our spiritual knowledge. We musn't be too disappointed when at times we fail. Providing we recognise the failure and sincerely try to do better next time, we will be making progress. The animal kingdom is a very good place to start.

By using our hard earned knowledge towards greater kindness and tolerance for animals, we lay sound foundations for the same attributes and progress towards the suffering human race. We must acknowledge that our pet animals show great tolerance towards us, at times they put us to shame – they are wonderful teachers for those who wish to learn. It is we who often exhibit so little tolerance and understanding of those around us – of both the human and animal species – who fail to learn the lessons of tolerance.

Anyone who has owned, been owned, loved and been loved by a pet dog will know the tolerance it will display towards our idiosyncrasies, carelessness and thoughtlessness. It will then display a very possessive *intolerance* towards a threat against *us*. Clearly they have no problem in deciding where motive and loyalties lie in the matter of tolerance. Only our own complicated and straggly thinking gives us the problem of deciding on our own motives. Our own selfishness is too often our real motive. Animals are not encumbered with selfishness in the same way – another lesson we could well learn from them on the road to tolerance – for the right reason, and the courage of *in*tolerance when a real need arises.

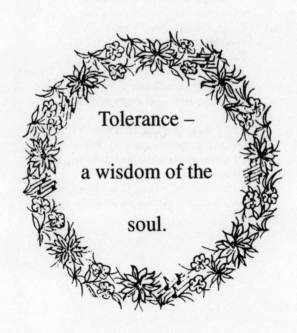

Tolerance –

a wisdom of the

soul.

BIRD OF PARADISE

Such wonders in the world we see,
Shrouded in mists of mystery,
From icy wastes to desert heat,
From wings and fins to pounding feet,
Or silent glade of flower and leaf
To stagger the mind in disbelief.

Large and small the wonders fly
To greet our ever watchful eye.
The majesty of a mighty tree,
The tiny insect wandering free,
The beauty of a flower in bloom,
Its colour, form and sweet perfume.

But nothing ever can compare
Or have a mystery quite so rare,
Or taunt our thoughts with fine display,
To teach us mortals how to pray,
With a heavenly name that will suffice
As a beautiful bird of paradise.

MOONBEAMS

Early this morning, one of our dogs asked to go outside, a very ordinary situation for any pet owner, but it demonstrated for me how the simple things of life can have enormous value, it reminded me that the humblest thoughts and actions play their parts towards this complicated life of ours. In the early morning silence, as I waited for a few minutes in the velvet darkness of a night that would shortly disappear, I felt again the wonder of life on earth, the mystery and beauty that is there for all who wish to see and know, the power of Spirit that surrounds us, tolerating with patience our own foolish exasperating ways.

There hung the crescent moon, tipped up to catch the rain our forefathers said, prophesying fine weather. Not far away it seemed, an enormous bright star. My book says we call it Venus, I call it the star of the East, for that is where the sun will later rise. The moon and star between them created such light that the other stars were dimmed into disappearance, but here and there another early riser added the small glow of electric light to the general scene.

Across the river other man-made lights glittered brightly, blue and orange, trembling with the vibration of the atmosphere – or was it anxiety for its comparison with the power and majesty of moon and star? They did seem puny even in their own quiet beauty, but had doubled their effect by reflection in the water.

The river flowed on as silently as the rest of this early morning world, to mingle with the pounding sea, just too far away to register its sounds of rhythmic power – the special wonder of the sea.

I stared across the valley at the uneven treetop edge of the wooded hill, dark picoting against the moon drenched sky. A wary pheasant stirred and called one startled note, an owl perching somewhere there in the quiet wood seemed to answer, and say "All is well", for the pheasant didn't call again.

Other creatures dwell within these woods, daily living out their lives according to God's plan, and unaware of the disturbance that can be created by the greediness of mankind.

They will learn of this later in the day, when the peace and mystery has flown on hasty wings before the farmers' guns and waving flags, while trusting pheasants that have been fed and fattened ready for this time of year fall helplessly from the sky to crash, fluttering their last goodbye, on the grass among the sheep that graze in innocence of their own much later fate. Peace and beauty will be replaced by fear and the ugliness that mankind perpetrates.

The rising sun, red and golden in its glory, reveals the chaos caused by man, shaming with its floodlight glow his own stupidity, searching out the darker corners of his mind and futile activities of his day. How the angels must weep to see the cruelty and confusions we create.

Yet here and there the gentle glow of kindness has always made its mark, struggling like a glow-worm's glimmer in the darkness of despair, to illuminate a better path of thought and action.

The plight of people and animals world-wide has alerted millions to the need for a change of attitude towards our environment. The sufferings of so many through the ages will not have been in vain if callous indifference is now gradually replaced by true compassion. Countless numbers of the human race become increasingly aware of this need, often prompted by the sight of suffering or experience of a kindness shown.

It is strange how the human being seems to insist on learning everything the hard way – bitter experience, when in fact there is so much to learn in easier ways. Man's natural curiosity guides him into learning much that is worthwhile towards his own progression. That same curiosity can also lead him along paths where the trees of knowledge bear no fruit for his present earthly existence and ill prepare him for the next, leaving him to guess and make unprovable assumptions, the truth of which would not help him in any case. Meanwhile, the precious gift of time that God has given him is being wasted, while the simple things of life could teach him so much more.

The smiles and tragedies of daily life are there for everyone to see and hear, the child that cries at some unseen fear of its own, or laughs at Grandad making funny faces. The sunrise and sunset, the falling pheasant betrayed by the hand that fed it, the injured hedgehog healed and nursed back to health by someone who simply cared. The sum total of the lessons that can be learnt in such simple ways causes the mind to boggle at the thought. The extent of kindness and compassion that can be created by such modest thinking, throws wide the doors of peace, tranquillity and love, and perhaps the easiest of lessons can be taught by the animals of the world.

Mankind has miserably failed to learn compassion towards his fellow man, only the few who have become aware of the need try to show a way by their own example, and often suffer as a consequence. In this pecking order of life, mankind makes little progress and the animal life gets nowhere at all, except in the isolated pockets of more advanced souls. If human beings, through recognition of the need to conserve their own environment, were to slightly change course and actively protect it and all life that it supports, then conscientiousness towards animals would automatically increase, and in the process greater caring and compassion towards people. A different path towards the same destination.

The sheer simplicity of it all demands attention, the uncomplicated logic of such thinking is there for all to see, but our habit in the world of people, of seeking for the complicated and relatively unobtainable, blinds us to the greater and more worthy knowledge that we could acquire from the simpler things of life, and this must inevitably include the animal kingdom, where much of their basic knowledge could be of such great value to mankind. Compassion is the route, unselfishness the vehicle, with peace and love at journey's end for all.

To work towards the relief of suffering of all kinds, is a noble occupation, and much needed action, but the only real cure for the maladies of cruelty, fear and pain is to prevent the conditions that cause them in the first place. This calls for spirituality of the mind on a world-wide scale. This can only be accomplished when individual people become aware of both the need and cure. No holding back because others remain blind to the cause, for this is a case of billions of particles making up the whole, like a field of buttercups and daisies, with all those petals, stamens, roots and leaves – a sight to behold in full bloom, but much to be done by worker bees and nature before the full glorious effect is seen. We are those workers. Spirit is the helping hand of nature, and the full result is yet to come, and every single person can play their part. Some will fail or refuse for a while to start, but this must be the spur for even greater effort and understanding on the part of those who have discovered the path towards spirituality of the mind, the road to God.

The moon that faded with the brightness of the sun did not fade at all, it was an illusion, for as it slipped from our own sight, it brightened the path for other souls in foreign parts, taking its message of hope to the other side of our world, that people there may also have the opportunity to learn from simplicity, the truth of spirituality – by the bright light of a crescent moon and its companion light – the star.

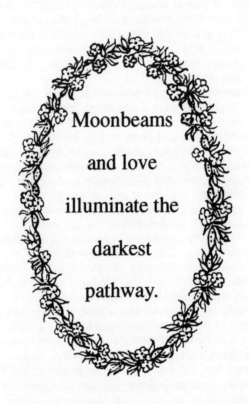

Moonbeams

and love

illuminate the

darkest

pathway.

THE DREAM

The human race can rightly seek its dream
  Of universal harmony and peace,
With nations joined as one great kindly team,
  That cruelty and pain shall one day cease.

When individual consciences are stirred,
  And ice floes never stained with the blood of seals,
And kindness joins in action undeterred,
  We'll see the light of love that it reveals.

When the raucous sound of markets turn to song,
  And flesh is never turned to dying gore,
And people learn to sort the right from wrong,
  Then callous thought and action is no more.

In future times the dog can have its day,
  The donkey, horse and cat be unafraid,
The outstretched hand will soothe all cares away,
  Never more in anger to be laid.

When starving children weep no more in pain,
  And life on earth is adequately fed,
Mankind can lift its guilty head again,
  When everyone receives their daily bread.

With seas no longer red from harpooned whales,
  And pesticides no longer killing butterflies,
With curlews flying free o'er moors and dales,
  Mankind can see its way to be more wise.

When peaceful badgers trundle through the leaves
    Unmolested by the cruelties of man,
And deer can browse in peace amongst the trees,
    Mankind is getting near to God's own plan.

When greedy slaughter bows its shameful head,
    With cruelty an echo from the past,
And evil thought is well and truly dead,
    The human race can find its dream at last.

A LAST WORD

I hope you have enjoyed this our fourth book and have found something of interest, a smile or two, maybe a few facts of which you were previously unaware. If you feel that I have put the case for animals in a way that will be advantageous to at least some of them, then I am satisfied. If you can also work towards their cause as a result of your reading here, then I am happy.

To those who may not be able to associate their ideas with those expressed here, I can only ask that you use this opportunity to look at the world through a different eye – one that would belong to a member of the animal kingdom, and maybe see ourselves for a moment as they see us.

If pain and despair are the criteria for giving help, then there are many calls upon our time and resources. There are millions of people out there begging for relief. I do not ask that they be forgotten or given second place to the animals. I ask that more compassion be engendered and fostered in human hearts and minds, to be shared amongst *all* life on earth wherever pain and fear demands it.

Mankind cannot hide behind illusions of superiority, for that is only in the dimension we call heaven – or the spirit world – names matter so very little. What really matters, is our knowledge and the way we use it. If we use it badly, heaven will weep, if we use it well then heaven will smile and the animals will thank us, for they too know a thing or two.

ORGANISATIONS
who are mentioned in the text of this book.

THE BAT CONSERVATION TRUST,   AIMS: To conserve bats and
The London Ecology Centre,   their habitats.
45 Shelton Street,
London, WC2H 9HJ
Tel. 071-240 0933

BEAUTY WITHOUT CRUELTY   AIMS: To produce cosmetics
  LTD., (B.W.C.),   without testing on
37 Avebury Avenue,   animals or using
Tonbridge,   animal tested
Kent, TN9 1TL   ingredients, and
Tel. 0732 365291   without the use of
                                                     slaughterhouse
                                                     or fish industry
                                                     by-products.

BRITISH UNION for the ABOLITION   AIMS: Campaigns against
  of VIVISECTION, (B.U.A.V.),   experiments on
16a Crane Grove,   animals.
London, N7 8LB
Tel. 071-700 4888

THE CATS PROTECTION LEAGUE,   AIMS: To rescue stray,
17 Kings Road,   unwanted cats and
Horsham,   kittens, rehabilitate
West Sussex, RH13 5PP   and rehome them,
Tel. 0403 261947   inform the public
                                                     of their needs, and
                                                     encourage the
                                                     neutering of cats not
                                                     required for breeding.

COMPASSION IN WORLD
  FARMING, (C.I.W.F.),
20 Lavant Street,
Petersfield,
Hants, GU32 3EW
Tel. 0730 642 08

AIMS: The abolition of
factory farming and
promoting kinder
treatment for all
farm animals.

CORNISH SHIRE HORSE CENTRE
  And OWL SANCTUARY,
Wadebridge,
Cornwall, PL27 7RA
Tel. 0841 540 276

AIMS: The breeding and
conservation of Shire
Horses and Barn
Owls.

FRAME,
Eastgate House,
34 Stoney Street,
Nottingham NG1 1NB
Tel. 0602 584740

AIMS: Researching
alternatives to
animal testing.

GREENPEACE,
Canonbury Villas,
London, N1 2PN
Tel. 071-354 5100

AIMS: To preserve or
recreate an
environment in which
living things,
including people, can
survive without threat
to their lives and
health.

HUMANE RESEARCH TRUST,
Brook House,
29 Bramhall Lane South,
Bramhall,
Cheshire, SK7 2DN
Tel. 061-439 8041

AIMS: To promote and
sponsor research
without the use of
animals.

INTERNATIONAL FUND FOR
     ANIMAL WELFARE (I.F.A.W.),
Tubwell House,
New Road,
Crowborough,
East Sussex, TN6 2QH
Tel. 0892 663374

AIMS: Tackles the
     problems of cruelty
     and abuse to animals,
     on a huge
     international scale.

LYNX,
P.O. Box 300,
Nottingham, NG1 5HN
Tel. 0602 403211

AIMS: To protect fur
     bearing animals,
     either wild or
     bred and kept in
     captivity.

MEN OF THE TREES,
Sandy Lane,
Crawley Down,
Crawley,
W. Sussex, RH10 4HS
Tel. 0342 712536

AIMS: To increase
     afforestation areas all
     over the world, and
     protect those already
     in existence.

MINIATURE PONY CENTRE,
Wormhill Farm,
North Bovey,
Nr. Newton Abbot,
Devon, TQ13 8RG
Tel. 0647 432400

AIMS: The breeding and
     preservation of
     Miniature Shetland
     Ponies.

NATIONAL CANINE DEFENCE
     LEAGUE,
1 Pratt Mews,
London, NW1 OAD
Tel. 071-388 0137

AIMS: To rescue dogs, to
     help them and
     prevent their
     suffering, and when
     possible to rehome
     them in kind homes.

THE NATIONAL SHIRE HORSE
  CENTRE,
Yealmpton,
Plymouth,
S. Devon. PL8 2EL
Tel. 0752 880268

AIMS: The preservation and breeding of the Shire Horse, and its presentation and promotion to the general public.

PEOPLE'S DISPENSARY FOR SICK
  ANIMALS, (P.D.S.A.),
Whitechapel Way,
Priorslee,
Telford,
Shropshire, TF2 9PQ
Tel. 0952 290999

AIMS: To provide free veterinary treatment for sick and injured pets of owners who qualify for the Society's free charitable service.

REDWINGS HORSE SANCTUARY,
Hill Top Farm,
Hall Lane,
Frettenham, Nr. Norwich,
Norfolk, NR12 7LT
Tel. 0603 737432

AIMS: The rescue and care of horses, ponies and donkeys that have been ill-treated and and neglected.

REINBOW'S END PONY RESERVE,
The Lodge,
Enmore, Bridgewater,
Somerset, TA5 2DU
Tel. 0278 671649

AIMS: To rescue and care for ponies that are victims of all kinds of cruelty and neglect, with an emphasis on saving foals from slaughter.

RIDING FOR THE DISABLED
  ASSOCIATION,
(Incorporating Driving),
Avenue "R",
National Agricultural Centre,
Kenilworth,
Warickshire, CV8 2LY
Tel. 0203 696510

AIMS: To provide the opportunity of riding and driving to disabled people who might benefit in their general health and wellbeing.

THE ROYAL SOCIETY FOR THE
  PROTECTION OF BIRDS (R.S.P.B.),
The Lodge,
Sandy,
Bedfordshire, SG19 2DL
Tel. 0767 680551

AIMS: The protection and
conservation of all
wild birds and their
natural habitat.

THE VEGETARIAN SOCIETY,
Parkdale,
Dunham Road,
Altrincham,
Cheshire, WA14 4QG
Tel. 061-928 0793

AIMS: To promote and
encourage cruelty-
free eating and
living.

THE V.W.T. BAT PROJECT,
Paignton Zoo,
Totnes Road,
Paignton,
Devon, TQ4 7EU
Tel. 0803 521064

AIMS: To promote bat
conservation and
research, and assist
county bat groups
and provide funding
for their activities
and for bats' roost
protection.

WHALE AND DOLPHIN
  CONSERVATION SOCIETY,
19a James Street West,
Bath,
Avon, BA1 2BT
Tel. 0225 334 511

AIMS: The conservation
and protection of
every known species
of whales, dolphins
and porpoises.

WORLD SOCIETY FOR THE
  PROTECTION OF ANIMALS
  (W.S.P.A.),
Park Place,
10 Lawn Lane,
London, SW8 IUD
Tel. 071-793 0540

AIMS: The reduction and
prevention of animal
suffering in all parts
of the world.

W.W.F. U.K. WORLD WIDE
FUND FOR NATURE,
Panda House,
Weyside Park,
Godalming,
Surrey, GU7 lXR
Tel. 0483 426444

AIMS: To conserve the world's natural resources and to prevent extinction of species and their habitats world wide. W.W.F. works through a combin-ation of field projects, policy work and public awareness campaigns.

SOME OTHER ORGANISATIONS
whose work for animals and the environment
is in keeping with the message of this book.

ANIMAL AID,
7 Castle Street,
Tonbridge,
Kent, TN9 lBH
Tel. 0732 364546

AIMS: Living without cruelty – the total eradication of all animal abuse, and to increase public awareness of the plight of animals.

THE ANIMAL WELFARE TRUST,
Headquarters: Tyler's Way,
Watford-By-Pass, Watford,
Herts, WD2 8HQ
Tel. 081-950 8215

AIMS: To rescue and rehome unwanted dogs, cats and all types of domestic animals, with a policy of never destroying a healthy animal.

Bristol, Avon & Som. Rescue Centre,
Heaven's Gate Farm,
West Henly, Langport,
Somerset, TA10 9BE
Tel. 0458 252656

BRITISH DIVERS MARINE LIFE
  RESCUE,
10 Maylan Road,
Corby,
Northants, NN17 2DR
Tel. 0536 201511

AIMS: The preservation and
rescue of all British
marine life.

THE CORNWALL DONKEY AND
  PONY SANCTUARY,
Lower Maidenland,
St. Kew, Bodmin,
Cornwall, PL30 3HA
Tel. 0208 84242

AIMS: To rescue and care
for ill-treated and
unwanted donkeys
and ponies, and offer
facilities for children
and adults to get to
know and understand
the animals and their
needs.

THE DONKEY SANCTUARY,
Sidmouth,
Devon, EX10 ONU
Tel. 0395 516391

AIMS: The rescue of ill-
treated donkeys and
providing them with
medical treatment
and care.

FARM ANIMAL WELFARE
  CO-ORDINATING EXECUTIVE
  (FAWCE),
Springhill House,
280 London Road,
Cheltenham, GL52 6HS
Tel. 0242 524 725

AIMS: To provide a
co-ordinating body
for various animal
welfare groups
towards improved
conditions for all
farm and food
animals, birds and
fish.

FRIENDS OF THE EARTH (FoE),
26-28 Underwood Street,
London, N1 7JQ
Tel . 071-490 1555

AIMS: Friends of the Earth opposes destruction of the environment and proposes constructive solutions. It informs the public, campaigns locally, nationally and internationally on a wide range of environmental issues.

HORSES AND PONIES
    PROTECTION ASSOCIATION
    (H.A.P.P.A.),
Happa House,
64 Station Road,
Padiham, Nr. Burnley,
Lancs. BB12 8EF
Tel. 0282 79138

AIMS: The protection of ponies and horses against all cruelty, being particularly concerned with the terrible transit conditions to which they are often exposed.

LEAGUE AGAINST CRUEL
    SPORTS,
83-87 Union Street,
London, SE1 lSG
Tel. 071-407 0979

AIMS: The abolition of blood sports.

NATIONAL FEDERATION OF
    BADGER GROUPS,
16 Ashdown Gardens,
Sanderstead, South Croydon,
Surrey, CR2 9DR

AIMS: To enhance the welfare, conservation and protection of badgers, their setts and habitats. To set up and support a network of badger protection groups and work closely with other wildlife protection bodies.

THE NATIONAL TRUST,
36 Queen Anne's Gate,
London, SW1H 9AS
Tel. 071-222 9251

AIMS: For places of historic interest or natural beauty, including sites that are environmentally important for wildlife.

THE ROYAL SOCIETY FOR
NATURE CONSERVATION
(R.S.N.C.)
The Green, Witham Park,
Waterside South,
Lincoln, LN5 7JR
Tel. 0522 544400

AIMS: To create a better future for Britain's wildlife.

THE WILDLIFE HOSPITAL TRUST
(Teaching Hospital),
Aston Road,
Haddenham, Aylesbury,
Buckinghamshire, HP17 8AF
Tel. 0844 292292

AIMS: To treat all sick or injured birds and wild animals and rehabilitate them back to the wild. The Trust also tries to pass on its knowledge and encourage other rehabilitators.

THE WOODLAND TRUST,
Autumn Park,
Dysart Road,
Grantham,
Lincolnshire, NG31 6LL
Tel. 0476 74297

AIMS: To acquire and conserve broadleaved woodland and create new woods for the benefit of wildlife and people.